Luiz tilted his head to one side, for all the world as though he was paying keen attention and actually listening to what she was suggesting.

"No."

"No? *No?* What do you mean *No?*" Holly looked at him in sudden confusion. She had exhausted all the options she could think of, so what exactly was he turning down? All of them? Didn't he know that there was nothing else on the table?

"Let me put it this way...as far as I am concerned, the only choice I have is to marry you. My child will be born legitimate. There's no other alternative. Rest assured that as far as money goes, you will be well taken care of. In fact, you could say that you will be rich beyond your wildest dreams."

Holly was staring at him as though he had just grown wings and was now informing her that he would be flying to the moon. She wasn't sure that she had quite heard correctly.

Marriage?

**All about the author…**
*Cathy Williams*

**CATHY WILLIAMS** was born in the West Indies and has been writing Harlequin® romances for some fifteen years. She is a great believer in the power of perseverance as she had never written anything before (apart from school essays a lifetime ago!), and from the starting point of zero has now fulfilled her ambition to pursue this most enjoyable of careers. She would encourage any would-be writer to have faith and go for it! She lives in the beautiful Warwickshire countryside with her husband and three children, Charlotte, Olivia and Emma. When not writing she is hard-pressed to find a moment's free time in between the millions of household chores, not to mention being a one-woman taxi service for her daughters' never-ending social lives. She derives inspiration from the hot, lazy, tropical island of Trinidad (where she was born), from the peaceful countryside of middle England and, of course, from her many friends, who are a rich source of plots and are particularly garrulous when it comes to describing Harlequin Presents heroes. It would seem, from their complaints, that tall, dark and charismatic men are way too few and far between! Her hope is to continue writing romance fiction and providing those eternal tales of love for which, she feels, we all strive.

**Other titles by Cathy Williams available in ebook:**

Harlequin Presents®

Harlequin Presents® Extra

# Cathy Williams

## THE SECRET CASELLA BABY

Recycling programs
for this product may
not exist in your area.

ISBN-13: 978-0-373-13148-8

THE SECRET CASELLA BABY

**Printed in U.S.A.**

# THE SECRET CASELLA BABY

# CHAPTER ONE

BEHIND THE WHEEL of his top-of-the-range silver sports car, Luiz Casella edged his foot down on the accelerator and felt the low, responsive growl of the vehicle as it leapt faster along the narrow country road. This was madness; he shouldn't be here, in the depths of a wintry, deserted Yorkshire countryside, pitting his ability to drive against nature's ability to stop him. On one side, endless fields, snow-covered, meandered out towards a horizon fast being consumed by darkness. On the other the bank rose steadily upwards, an icy mass of unforgiving rock that would shatter his car if he made the mistake of getting too close.

Luiz knew that. He also knew that he had to do this, he had to work this crazy, maddening grief out of his system somehow, and he couldn't think of a better way of doing it than by dicing with death a million miles away from the well-ordered, clinical sanity of his London penthouse.

It had been nearly a year since his father had died. A strapping, adventurous man in his early sixties, Mario Casella had been alive, strong and vibrant one day, nagging his son that it was time to settle down, threatening to leave Brazil and fly to London to persuade him. The next, he had been a crumpled, lifeless body barely identifiable in the ruins of the small light aeroplane which he had been determined to master.

Luiz had taken the call from his sobbing mother and had returned immediately to Brazil where he had risen to the challenges awaiting him. As the only son, he had become immediate head of the family. He handled everything, from the funeral arrangements to the sudden crisis within his father's company caused by his death. He juggled the managing of his own companies from a distance.

He was the reassuring rock to which his mother, his three sisters, various assorted relatives and a number of business associates had turned. He had not allowed any poisonous thread of weakness to corrupt his remorseless, single-minded determination to do what he knew he had to do. He had appointed the necessary people to run his father's company and made sure they knew that one slip up, and they would be answerable to him. He had arranged for the family mansion to be sold because his mother couldn't face the prospect of living there without her husband. He had found somewhere equally luxurious but much smaller in the same cul de sac as one of his sisters. He had quietly put some of the more sentimental mementoes into storage where they would rest until the time came when his mother would be strong enough to face looking at them. He had done all this without shedding a tear.

When he had returned to London, months later, it was to resume the running of his own personal empire. He threw himself into a work routine that would have crippled any normal human being. He began a ferocious programme of buy-outs that saw his personal wealth increase ten fold.

The latest buy-out of a failing electronics company in Durham had given him the first opportunity he had had to release some of the savage energy that had been burning a hole inside him since his father's death. He had taken advantage of it, arranging for his car to be at the airport and allowing himself a few hours' respite from his gruelling work agenda to drive back down to London.

He hadn't intended to be distracted by country lanes but the challenge of those small, deserted icy roads had been irresistible. He had switched off his GPS navigation and now here he was.

In the failing light, he could see the first light glimmers of snow beginning to fall like translucent powder, necessitating the windscreen wipers. He had switched off his phone, switched off the radio, and all he could hear was the deep, sepulchral silence of winter battling against the low roar of his powerful car.

Had his father felt any pain before he'd died? He would have known that death was imminent as his plane had plummeted out of the sky, like a bird with its wings catastrophically snapped. What had been his thoughts?

Surely no regrets? His father had been the finest example of what a clever man possessed of boundless energy and imagination could achieve. He had taken himself away from his impoverished background and worked his way steadily upwards until he had finally been able to reside in that rarefied place where money was no object. He had married his childhood sweetheart, who had stood by him every inch of the way, and together they had had four children. No; there would surely have been no regrets there.

Luiz liked to think that there was comfort to be derived from that but no amount of mental acrobatics could stifle the pain of the unanswered questions, or knowing that the single one man he had truly admired was gone for ever from his life.

His hands tightened on the wheel. A searing ache began uncoiling in the very pit of his stomach. He clenched his jaw, pressed harder on the accelerator, and in the blink of an eye that unforgiving face of rock was bearing down towards him.

Luiz reacted in a split second, veering away from it, feeling it brush against the side of his car, hearing the shriek of protesting metal against immovable stone, then his car was spinning out of control and hurtling across the country lane, now shrouded in darkness, out towards the expanse of fields.

The impact left him momentarily dazed but his airbag had done its thing and the strength of the vehicle had weathered the crash better than he could have hoped for. But he was still winded and in a bad way as he manoeuvred himself out of the car and dragged himself as far away from it as possible. He was running on a full tank and there was every chance that the thing would go up in flames. Remain too close, and it would take him along for the ride.

But walking was going to be a problem. He gingerly felt his leg and the gash running along it. He was without a coat, in the middle of nowhere and there was not a single light in sight. To make matters worse, the snow had decided to gather momentum. The powdery dust was fast turning into fat snowflakes that began settling on his hair, his useless work trousers—lovingly hand-tailored but totally inappropriate in falling snow—the designer jumper which would be soaked through in under half an hour and on the fields stretching as far as the eye could see.

Gritting his teeth, he began making his way slowly back towards the road. He would just have to take things from there. He had his mobile phone and, whilst he was fully aware that the network in these parts would probably be severely challenged, sooner or later he would be able to pick up a signal.

And, hey; a grim smile flitted across his dark, aristocratic face. This physical pain, after months of putting a cap on the far uglier pain of his emotions, almost felt good…

* * *

Had he but known it, less than two miles away, Holly George, in the act of doing her routine check of her cherished animal sanctuary, heard the distant scream of the car crash and instantly stilled, cocking her head to listen a little harder.

She had grown up in this wild, spectacular terrain and she knew it intimately. She knew its changing moods, its unexpectedly graceful nooks and crannies and she knew its sounds. Especially in the depths of February when the silence could be bottomless.

She snapped shut the gate on Buster the donkey, a new addition, and hurried inside the stone cottage, taking off her woolly hat in the process so that long, curly fair hair the colour of vanilla spilled over her shoulders and rippled down her back.

*Someone's come off the road.* There was no question of it. For a few seconds she debated whether to call Andy, her partner at the sanctuary, but then dismissed the idea before it had chance to form. Andy had left early for a cookery course in town, hosted by his favourite chef. He had been looking forward to it for the past three weeks and she wasn't about to ruin his good time by dragging him out on a search and rescue mission.

Ben Firth would gladly have got his boys together and headed out with their fire trucks, and Abe, the local doctor, would have rustled up the ambulance, but where would they head? The funny thing with sound around here was that the echoes of it could literally have originated anywhere. But she knew this place like the back of her hand. She would be able to pin point where the crash had happened and get there much faster than Ben and his crew, who were based over fifteen miles away, or Abe for that matter, who was closer but not by much.

Holly George was only twenty-six years old but she was

sensible, practical and used to the harsh winters delivered every year in remote Yorkshire. Sometimes it occurred to her that sensible and practical were not very feminine traits, which might have accounted for the lack of men pounding on her front door begging for a date. But whenever she thought of leaving her beloved animal sanctuary and moving to one of the big cities with bright lights, clubs, bars and all those other things her friends kept telling her she needed, she literally felt ill.

Her father had been a farmer and she had always lived around animals. Her body clock was primed for early mornings and the onset of spring was always a reminder of the wonders of lambing. Her father had died years ago, shortly after she had turned eighteen, and she had reluctantly sold the farm, knowing that managing the extensive acres of arable would be out of the question, even with a great deal of help. In its place, she had sunk what she had made on the farm into the animal sanctuary which now occupied her time. Once she had paid the bills there was precious little money left, but she had her cottage, with its grumbling heating system and eccentric plumbing, and she didn't owe a thing on it. She had bought it outright.

But the question of time passing her by while her friends lived it up and tried to drag her out was still the occasional wrinkle in an otherwise uncomplicated existence. She had only ever had one serious boyfriend. James had been training to be a vet and they had met at one of the many courses she enjoyed attending to better her understanding of how to look after the animals she rescued. He had been giving the lecture as part of his coursework and she had immediately warmed to his evident nervousness. They had got chatting and, when their relationship had ended after a year and a half, they had remained firm friends.

Personally, Holly thought that she might very well have

missed her chance because she couldn't imagine that there was anyone more on her wavelength than James had been. But he had been transferred south and had just not been able to tolerate the physical distance. She often wondered whether she should have tried harder because time moved on and…

She paused by the front door to reach for the keys to her ancient four-wheel drive and glanced at the reflection in the little brass mirror attached to the hooks for the keys.

This face would never suit the bright lights, she decided, and neither would this body. She lacked the fashionable angular lines that looked good in tight clothes and she had never quite cracked the art of make-up. The bright blue eyes staring back at her were rarely adorned with mascara or eye-liner. Her face was soft, gentle, too feminine to be sexy.

She turned away without dwelling further on her physical drawbacks.

Outside the snow was getting heavier, and she knew that there was no time for second thoughts, but her car was extremely sturdy and as she switched on the engine it let out its usual reassuring rumble.

There were several roads and lanes she could have taken but she unerringly went for the right one. It was the most hazardous. In the past four years, three accidents had taken place on one of the bends that forked left without warning. If that wasn't the site of the car crash, then she would have no difficulty in picking up another lane.

Making her way through the snow, she spotted the car as soon as the narrow road allowed her an unimpeded view straight ahead. It was skewed into the field at an angle that made her urge her old car on faster. Snow was already gathering on it and even from a distance she could see that it was a complete write off.

She was squinting to make out the detail in the beam of

her headlights and very nearly missed the figure at the side of the road, barely standing and signalling to her to stop.

A man, on his own, and not kitted out for the weather; she could make that much out as she carefully pulled to the side of the road.

'Is there anyone else with you?' Holly asked anxiously, hurrying over and wrapping her arm around his waist. Half-slumped, she was conscious of the firmness of muscle and the weight of someone much taller than her.

'Just me.' Luiz ground his teeth to bite back the agony of his leg as they hobbled, clutching each other, to a car that looked like the left-over relic from another century.

'Your car…'

'Completely destroyed.'

'I'll arrange for someone to come out and fetch it.'

'Forget it. I couldn't give a damn about it.'

Holly wondered who couldn't give a damn about something as expensive as a car. Letting him go for the second it took to open the passenger door, she felt the brush of his body as he settled into the seat with a grimace of pain.

A thousand questions were running through her head. Which would be the quickest route to the hospital? He was standing and he was talking, but was he seriously injured? Should she be asking him about any family members she could contact? Should she do some sort of routine check to make sure that he wasn't concussed?

She raised her eyes, one of those questions already forming on her lips, and was skewered to the spot by the sort of spectacular good looks that just made her want to stare and keep on staring. His eyes were deep and dark and the snow glistened on short black hair and on a lean-boned face that was breathtakingly, uncompromisingly masculine. He was exotically foreign, his skin the colour of burnished gold. Her heart set up a tempo that was so alien to her that she could feel bright, flustered colour invade her cheeks.

'Are you comfortable?' she managed to ask in a staccato voice that was very different from her usually calm, unruffled tone.

'As comfortable as I can be with a leg that's been ripped open.'

At which Holly roused herself out of her stupor sufficiently to look at the bloodied trousers and she gave a little gasp of horror.

'You need the hospital.' She switched on the engine. The snow was falling more heavily and it took her a little while before her tyres could grip the tarmac.

'How far is it?'

'Quite far.' She had to fight the temptation to sneak one more look at that face. 'You're not from around here, are you?'

'Is it so easy to tell?' Luiz rested his head against the window and stared at her profile. He had the strangest feeling that he had crashed, died and gone to heaven, because she was the most angelic thing he had ever seen in his life. Her skin was as smooth as satin, her enormous eyes were the pure blue of cornflowers; her hair, flyaway blonde, cascaded down her back and over her shoulders in natural, wild disarray, so different from the poker-straight hairstyles that were everywhere in London. The pain in his leg was now a steady throb, pulsing underneath the trousers.

'You're wearing the wrong clothes. No one would venture out in weather like this without a few more layers. Look, it's going to be impossible to get you to the hospital, but I can call and find out whether they can send a rescue helicopter for you.'

Luiz thought of the carelessness that had landed him in

this mess and flushed darkly. 'I can handle it myself. There's no need for a rescue helicopter.'

'You're kidding.'

When she smiled, her cheeks dimpled. He had never seen anything like it.

'I haven't even introduced myself,' Holly said shyly. 'I'm Holly George.'

'Well, Holly George,' Luiz murmured, 'What were you doing out on the roads in this weather? Won't your parents be wondering where you've gone?'

'I live on my own. Not very far away, as a matter of fact. I heard you crash so I jumped in my car and drove here. I was going to alert Ben and Abe but it would have taken them ages. That's the problem with living in such a remote place; if you run into trouble in the depths of winter, you just have to keep your fingers crossed that you can hold out for a few hours.'

'Who are Ben and Abe?'

'Oh, Ben's in charge of the fire station and old Abe is the local doctor.'

'It all sounds very cosy.'

'What were you doing on those roads?'

'Getting rid of some of my demons.'

Holly glanced across at him at that intriguing statement but his eyes were veiled and she instinctively knew that he was not a man who would expand on anything if she chose to ask him a direct question. How did she know that? Where had that gut feeling come from?

'Those lights up ahead…' She turned off the main road and felt the familiarity of the grounds surrounding her cottage. 'My cottage is there. I…I run an animal sanctuary.'

'You do what?'

'I run an animal sanctuary. You can just make out the buildings over there; they're heated and covered. We have about fifty animals. Dogs, cats, two horses, a donkey… Last year we even had a pair of llamas, but fortunately they were taken in by a children's farm.'

'Cats…horses…a donkey…' He had stepped into another world. This was so far beyond his realm of understanding that he could have been conversing with someone from another planet.

'What do you do?' Holly asked. 'I mean, what's your job?'

'My job…' They were pulling up in front of a small stone cottage, brightly lit. She turned to him and for a second his breath caught at the sight of her open, smiling heart-shaped face. He noticed details that had escaped his attention. For instance, not only were her eyes the bluest he had ever seen, but her eyelashes were incongruously dark and her mouth was full and beautifully defined. The fingers lightly gripping the steering wheel were slender, smooth and free of any rings. In fact, she wore no jewellery. Her clothes were basic, practical, unfashionable—jeans, a jumper over which she had flung a very worn, olive-green oilskin, wellies and a woollen hat with a Christmas motif. She was the least artificial person he could remember seeing in a long time.

'And your name; what's your name? Hang on, I'll come round your side and help you out and we can have a look at your injury and decide what to do. I have a lot of first-aid stuff and if it's superficial I can probably deal with it.'

Holly found that she was as tense as violin wire as once again that very masculine body was leaning against her, weighing her down even though she knew that he was doing his best to put as little pressure on her as he could. As always when she was nervous, she chattered as they walked very slowly through the snow towards the front door, and once in to the kitchen where he sat heavily on one of the pine chairs at her kitchen table.

This was just the sort of decor that Luiz loathed: lots of

rustic touches and one of those enormous ranges that did very little, as far as he was concerned, aside from take up useful space. The tiles on the floor were old, as old as the weathered rug underneath the pine table. Against one wall, a dresser was home to a variety of mismatched plates which fought for space alongside little framed pictures and various bric-a-brac of the sort guaranteed to have any interior designer worth her salt gnashing her teeth in frustration.

And yet...

He watched as she bustled, fetching a first-aid kit from one of the cupboards, not even looking at him directly as she concentrated on the gash on his leg.

'You'll have to help me get the trousers off,' he murmured and she hurriedly waved aside the suggestion.

Get his trousers off? Holly didn't think that her blood pressure could take it. His presence filled her small kitchen like no one else's ever had. However hard she tried to divert her eyes, they just kept coming back to him, big, muscular and indecently good-looking.

'I'll cut them. It's better that way.'

She knelt in front of him and Luiz felt the thrust of an erection that was so strong and so unexpected that he had to draw his breath in sharply. What was it about her? She had no sharp edges, no bony elbows, thin arms or stick legs. She was soft and rounded and he could see the shape of her full breasts even in the faded jeans and even more faded jumper, as seductive as ripe fruit.

As she gently began cutting away the trouser leg, apologising about ruining the lovely cloth, his head was suddenly filled with images of her naked in front of him, offering herself to him. He fidgeted and Holly looked up immediately.

'Have I hurt you?'

He wondered how she would react if he told her exactly what was hurting him at this moment in time.

'You're very brave. You must tell me if I hurt you. It's bound to but...'

She hurried off, to return seconds later with a glass of water and some tablets.

'Painkillers. Very strong. They'll help.' She could feel her skin tingling as he rested his dark eyes on her flushed face. It was strange, but when he looked at her she got the funniest feeling that she was being caressed.

'So you haven't told me your name...' Once again at the task of slitting the trousers, trying to ignore the strong legs slowly being revealed with their dark hair which was somehow so aggressively masculine, she launched into jumpy chatter.

'Ah, yes. Luiz. Luiz...Gomez.' He hoped that the head gardener who had been in charge of the grounds of the family house in Brazil would forgive him appropriating his surname, but suddenly it seemed a good idea. Here, with this woman kneeling at his feet, in surroundings so far removed from those to which he was accustomed, he would be a different person. Just for a few hours. He would no longer be a workaholic, driven by demons, in charge of an empire in which there was no time-out clause built in. There was no sin in seeking a little respite from the brutal reality of his life, was there?

'Luiz... Where are you from?'

'I live in London, as a matter of fact, but I come from Brazil.' He smiled at her delighted expression and relaxed as she chattered away about the places she would love to see one day. Her fingers were nimble and she worked quickly, explaining that he would need to see a doctor, would probably need antibiotics but it wasn't too bad, she would make sure she cleaned it thoroughly...

She laughed when he asked her whether she had been a

girl guide and he enjoyed the sound of her laughter. He felt he might like to hear it more often.

'I could stitch you up,' she told him. 'But I'm not sure whether you would be willing to trust me to do that. If not, I can bandage you up until we can get you to a doctor.'

Luiz half-murmured that when it came to being stitched up there had been a fair few women who had attempted the exercise.

'Is there somewhere I could stay out here?' he asked, looking around him as if he might just spy a cosy tavern at the bottom of the garden. Already his mind was moving ahead. Time out; this was the tonic he needed. A place where no one could find him, with a woman who had no agenda and to whom he would be no more than an injured stranger. The wealthy and powerful Luiz Casella could have a bit of peace and quiet. The man over whom women fawned could step back and luxuriate in the novelty of knowing that the health of his bank account was not a contributing factor.

And, of course, out here...

He feasted his eyes on her luscious curves, her achingly pretty face, which went pink every time he looked at her.

Holly blushed and laughed again as she straightened up, pleased with the job she had done. She was used to dealing with injuries. He was probably bruised on other parts of his body as well. She couldn't help admiring his stoicism. Not only was he fantastically good-looking, but he wasn't a complainer.

'The nearest bed and breakfast is at least twenty miles away. You couldn't have picked a worse spot to come off the road,' she said ruefully. 'I'll fix you something to eat and make up the spare room. You can stay here, if you like. At least overnight, until we can get you to a hospital.'

'I won't be needing a hospital.' Luiz thought that he couldn't have picked a better place to come off the road. He didn't know what it was about her, but already he felt calmer than he had in a long time.

'And you still haven't told me what you do. Or if I should get in touch with someone to tell them about your accident. A wife, perhaps…?'

Luiz could recognise a leading question when he heard one and he smiled slowly. 'No wife,' he murmured. 'No girl-friend. No one to contact.' He watched as she busied herself fixing them something to eat. The cupboards were hand-painted, cream and dark green. The tiles above the range cooker depicted children's drawings of various animals. It was warm in the kitchen and she pulled off the sweater so that she was down to a long-sleeved tee-shirt which clung faithfully to all her curves and to breasts which were as abundant as he had suspected. She was chattering, although he wasn't one hundred percent paying attention to what she was saying.

He knew that he was making all the right noises, and when finally she sat at the kitchen table with food in front of them—eggs and bacon and some of the best bread he had ever eaten—he knew that he was asking all the right questions.

He asked about the sanctuary, about how it was funded, about the details of how it was run, where the animals came from, the success rate at rehousing them.

She had an open, expressive face. She gesticulated excit-edly when she talked about her animals. They all had names. They tried to raise money locally to keep going. Person-ally, he thought that it all sounded like a lot of hard work for no profit, but he enjoyed looking at her enthusiasm. He couldn't remember being as enthusiastic as she was when he was closing his deals, which were usually worth mil-lions. He was tempted to offer her a substantial amount of money, a thank you for saving his life, but, having told her that he was little more than a travelling salesman, that possibility was ruled out.

'I might have to stay here slightly longer than a night,' he finally said as she rose to clear their dishes and Holly threw him an anxious glance over her shoulder.

'Won't your boss mind?' she asked, concerned. 'Things are so tough in the economy nowadays…I hope your job won't be under threat because you have to take time off.' When he said *stay here,* did he mean stay *here?* In her *house?* Or stay somewhere locally until he was fully recovered? She thought of him in her house and a guilty thrill of pleasure rippled through her. He was just the most interesting guy she had ever met, willing to listen to what she had to say and informative on all his responses.

'I think I'll be able to wing it on that score,' Luiz murmured. For a second, he felt a twinge of guilt at his creative manipulation of the truth but it didn't last long. He reasoned that she would be intimidated had she known the extent of his influence, power and wealth. She would respond far more quickly and openly to a travelling salesman type, someone safe and unthreatening.

'So getting back to you staying here…' Holly said uncertainly. 'I'm not sure what you mean, exactly…'

'Of course, I would insist on paying you. You could consider yourself the most convenient bed and breakfast, and I assure you, you would be generously compensated. In fact, you can name your price. I…I'm quite sure my boss would not hesitate to make whatever generous donation you might want towards your animal sanctuary.'

'I wouldn't dream of taking money from you!' Holly was horrified that he might think her so mercenary that she would try and charge him for what anyone else would have done in her situation.

'Even though, from all accounts, your animals don't exactly pay the bills?' Luiz was enjoying the unexpected novelty of this situation more and more. He couldn't think of a single woman who wouldn't have taken money from him. In fact, he was quite accustomed to lavishing presents on his women: diamonds, pearls, cars, holidays… Naturally, had she known the extent of his personal fortune, she would not have hesitated to take advantage of his generosity. He knew enough about women to be sure on that count. Her scruples would only have kicked in at the thought of depriving a struggling salesman who might or might not be in danger of losing his job.

'I know a bit about computers…' He had to conceal a smile when he said that, for he owned several IT companies and probably knew more about the workings of computers than most of the people he employed. 'Do you have a website? Because I could set one up for you…'

Not only did he not complain, not only was he interested in what she did, not only was he the perfect gentleman in offering to compensate her for her simple act of kindness, but here he was, doing his best to make himself useful! He just seemed to know everything. Perhaps computers were his thing.

'The main thing is that you get better,' she told him firmly. 'Would you like some tea? Coffee? And then I'll show you up to your bedroom. In the morning, I'll get in touch with Abe. The snow doesn't seem to be getting any heavier. He has a Jeep. He should be able to make it out here.'

'Are you always this upbeat?' Luiz wondered aloud and she favoured him with one of those smiles that he found strangely transfixing.

'I have a lot to be thankful for. This place, a job I love, lots of friends…' She placed the cafetière on the table along with two mugs and some milk and sugar. 'I no longer have my parents. My mother died when I was a kid, and my dad died a few years ago, but I like to think that they were very happy…'

'And that works for you?' Luiz's mouth twisted cynically at her innocent, sunny acceptance of what he, personally, had found unacceptable—of the event which, in a strange way, accounted for him sitting right here in this kitchen with a woman the likes of whom he had never known existed.

'Of course it does. What did you mean when you said that you were getting rid of some of your demons?'

Had anyone else asked him that question, Luiz would have shot them down with a glance, but as he stared into those sympathetic blue eyes, he felt that ache in his gut uncoil again.

He told her: he was just Luiz Gomez, a travelling salesman, allowed, for a brief window in time, to reveal his feelings. It wasn't easy. He was not a man given to sharing or confiding. When you were the power house, the person shouldering the responsibility and running the show, confiding about anything to anyone was not a desirable thing to do. It was a sign of weakness and, as one of those kings of the concrete jungle, weakness was not allowed.

But she made a damned good listener. He forgot about his leg, the incipient aches all over his body, his wrecked car, and at the end of an hour he had made his mind up.

Holly George was going to be his lover.

# CHAPTER TWO

HOLLY LOOKED AT the little wrought-iron table with matching chairs on the stone flagged patio which overlooked the open fields at the back of her cottage and felt a little knot of nervousness and excitement. She had laid everything out neatly. The bottle of wine—from the supply which was permanently re-stocked by Luiz, who was fussy with his alcohol—was chilling in the wine cooler. A dish of crudités was covered over, as were the little homemade savoury cheese biscuits. Midges; flies; they always came out in summer and it was still very warm, even though it was nearly six-thirty in the evening.

Any minute now, Luiz would be arriving in his taxi, and after nearly a year and a half she would still feel that giddy craving that always overwhelmed her the second she laid eyes on him.

This weekend, though, was going to be different. Holly smoothed her hands over her summer dress and hurried inside to hover by the window in the front room.

A wave of dizziness washed over her and she suspected that it was the heat. Recently, she had been prone to such waves of dizziness. It was an extremely and unusually hot summer. All her animals were lethargic. Her chickens, which usually pestered her by the kitchen door in search of scraps, took themselves off to shadier spots. Even her assortment of

dogs was less interested in running around than finding a
cosy niche underneath the nearest tree where they could lie,
tongues lolling, dreaming about running around.

She was lethargic. For the past three weeks, getting out
of bed in the mornings had been a struggle. Normally up
with the larks, she had found herself yearning to lie in a
couple of times and she had had to make a mammoth effort to get going.

Yorkshire, she had told Luiz, wasn't designed for searing
temperatures. It was designed for the cool, bright colours of
spring, the chill of autumn russets or the breathtaking cold
of a winter wonderland. Luiz had laughed and told her that
she should get some air-conditioning installed in her cottage
and she wouldn't feel so uncomfortable in the heat.

She teased him about his practicality. She told him that he
needed to cultivate some romance, but in truth their personalities blended beautifully together. She would never have
believed that after that initial meeting, when she had first
looked at him and concluded that he was just the most spectacular guy she had ever seen, he would come to fill her
world, all the corners of it.

They only ever met at weekends. She couldn't leave her
animals and he couldn't get time away from his job, which
she assumed took him travelling all over the country, selling all that computer stuff which made her glaze over whenever she thought too hard about it. But the time they spent
together was so intense, so vibrantly, wildly alive, that she
couldn't confess to having a second's doubt that he was just
the best thing that had ever happened to her.

He was her lover, her soul mate. He was the guy she knew
she could share everything with, from the small things, bits
and pieces of local gossip, to the really big things like when
some of the shelters had lost their roofs the year before in
a snow storm and the bank had been digging its heels in

about lending her the amount she needed to repair them to the standard she wanted. Well, Luiz had sorted it all out for her, and in fact had managed to talk the bank manager into lending her enough to really bring the whole sanctuary up to an incredibly high standard, far better than she could ever have imagined.

Plus, he had looked through all her deeds and papers and found a stash of cash sitting in an unused account dating back to the original sale of the farm. With the accumulated interest over the years, she hadn't even had to pay for any of the refurbishments. He was her rock.

As they did every time she thought of him, her fingers rested lovingly on the tiny red pendant he had given her the previous Christmas as a present before he had returned to Brazil—for, as he had told her, ten days of agony without the bliss of seeing her for the weekend. Her eyes had welled up at the present, because he had remembered her once telling him that rubies were her favourite stones, but he had waved aside her thanks and vaguely assured her that it was just a great copy, nothing to get all worked up about.

Over time, he had lavished her with a number of such great copies of precious jewellery. He knew a guy who knew a guy who could work magic when it came to terrific reproductions, he had told her. In return, she had given him little things she picked up at the craft fairs she occasionally went to. She had knitted him a sweater because his sweaters were far too thin—London sweaters, she had laughed, only useful for London winters. She had bought him a first edition of a book he had mentioned liking which she had found in an antique-book shop in an out-of-the-way village near Middlesbrough.

She smiled at the memory of how concerned he had been at the extravagance, but in truth, ever since he had set up that website, the finances of the place had never been so good.

Donations more than kept them going and there were now a couple of really generous anonymous online donors who almost single-handedly ensured that the sanctuary was in tip-top condition with money to spare.

Lost in her daydreams, she started at the sound of the door knocker and she was already succumbing to the thrill of anticipation as she pulled open the door.

'I couldn't get here fast enough...' Luiz kicked the door shut behind him and pulled her into his arms. En route, he had rolled up the sleeves of his shirt and his tie was stuffed into his trouser pocket. In weather like this, it would have made sense to have changed into something cooler before boarding his helicopter, but as always the need to see her was so urgent that he just couldn't bring himself to take time out to return to his apartment and change.

In fact, it was a source of continual gratification that he had use of a helicopter. Had he been obliged to take the train and a taxi, which he knew she assumed he did, he would have gone mad during the journey. Hell, no woman had ever been able to hold his attention for the length of time that she had and now he buried his head in her hair, breathing in her unique, gloriously womanly scent.

'There's wine outside.' Holly's laughter caught on a breath of intoxicating desire as he pushed her back to the wall and teased open the small buttons at the front of her dress.

'The wine will have to wait.' Luiz half-groaned. 'I've been thinking of nothing but this since I got into that taxi. Why the hell have you worn something with a thousand buttons, Holly? Are you trying to drive me crazy?'

'I'm not wearing a bra, though...'

'Then it's a good thing you answered the door to me,' Luiz growled possessively. 'Because that's something for my eyes only...' He couldn't get the buttons undone fast enough. His impulse was just to rip the dress open, but he knew that she would fret about the cost and he would be impotent to replace it. Eventually, the buttons were undone to the waist and he peeled the dress aside so that he could feast his eyes on her wondrous breasts.

Breathing unevenly, he flung his head back, nostrils flared, eyes half-closed before cupping those breasts in his big hands and rubbing the pads of his thumbs over the distended, swollen peaks of her large, circular nipples. He could have taken her right here, standing in the hallway, with her pressed up against the wall. Instead, he swept her off her feet and carried her into the front room where at his instigation, and with a great deal of persuasion, she had accepted the gift of an enormous sofa from him, big enough to take them both and essential, he had said, to cater for the times when they just couldn't make it to the bedroom. Which was often. He deposited her on the sofa now and stood up to remove his shirt.

Holly adored the hunger in his eyes. From the very beginning, unused to such naked desire, she had revelled in the way he made her feel: sexy, beautiful and very, very necessary. He went up in flames the second he touched her, he had told her, and she believed him because she could see the proof of it in his eyes. She pushed herself up and tugged down the zip of his trousers. His erection was big, bold and barely restrained by the boxers. She wriggled her hand to touch his arousal and he covered her hand with his and held it still.

'Don't,' he commanded in a strangled voice. 'Not unless you want to see me react like a horny teenager who has never had sex!'

Holly laughed and ignored him. The very first time they had made love, she had nervously wondered whether she had done all right. He was a man of infinite experience. She had known that the second he had trailed his finger along her cheek and down to her collarbone, watching her with a half-smile as she had shivered and shuddered and wondered whether she was doing the right thing.

That had been on his third day of sharing the cottage with her. His curiosity about her had been thrilling and insistent. And she had been bowled over by his confidence, his easiness, his wit, his intelligence. She had been ripe for the taking and she had loved every second of it.

'Tell me,' he had murmured softly, washing away the dregs of her hesitation all that time back, 'What could be wrong about this?' And he had teased her body with a sexy, feathery touch until it had felt as though it would go up in flames. He had taken his time and she had been swept away on a tide of passion. There had been no chance of her finding anything to cling to, no chance of common sense pulling her back to safety. Every expectation she had ever had of a normal life with a normal guy doing normal things and progressing down a normal route had been turned on its head and she hadn't regretted any of it for a minute.

She was no longer insecure about touching him, not like that very first time. He made her feel wonderfully, deliciously needed. She touched his pulsating erection with the delicate tip of her tongue and he groaned and shuddered.

'I can't wait… Get your clothes off.' He watched feverishly as she wriggled out of the annoying dress and the lacy underwear. He had introduced her to that concept the very first time he had returned to see her, only days after he had left: lacy underwear to replace the sensible cotton briefs. She had made a token protest but it hadn't lasted long. Even she could see how outrageously sexy the tiny bits of lace made her look. Sometimes, he would strip her down to that lacy underwear and tease her through the lace with his tongue until she was on fire for him.

That wouldn't be happening tonight. Not when he could barely keep a lid on his own uncontrolled libido.

She was divinely sexy lying on the bed with her hair rippling around her in waves of vanilla, caramel and gold. She let her legs drop open so that he could see the seductive details of her womanhood and he stilled in the process of pulling off his shirt when her fingers lightly touched herself. Her amazing eyes were half-closed but he knew that she was watching him, enjoying his reaction to what she was doing. He ripped the last two buttons of his shirt and subsided on the bed next to her.

'If you want to touch something...' He firmly guided her hand away from herself and back towards his erection. 'Then you can touch me!' He slid his fingers along her wetness and loved the feel of her moisture that made them slippery.

'We should be talking,' Holly whispered unevenly as insistent waves of pleasure began swelling inside her as he continued to stroke and rub between her legs.

'You'd be shocked if I didn't walk through that front door and grab you,' Luiz said with masculine satisfaction. 'You can't resist me.'

'You are *so* egotistic, Luiz Gomez!'

'Just reporting on what your body's telling me. Right now, you're hot and wet and those are definitely not the signs of a woman who wants to talk...' To emphasise his point, he straddled her in one easy movement and, on cue, she arched back, offering her breasts to him and closing her eyes as he began the languorous process of exploring every inch of them.

He could spend hours teasing and playing with her breasts. He loved everything about them. He had long given up asking himself how he could ever have gone out with women who weren't as generously built as the woman who was now writhing underneath him.

Holly's breathing was fast and interspersed with small little moans of satisfaction as he licked and nibbled. She half-opened her eyes to gaze lovingly at his dark head. When he nudged at her with his erection, she slipped into a bubble of pure ecstasy, and as he thrust forcefully in she was swept away. Their bodies moved in perfect harmony. She was already so excited that she could feel her orgasm building as he continued to push into her but she had learned to hold off until she could feel them both at the same point.

It came quickly, then she let herself go. Her moans became cries until her mind and body parted company and she was no longer capable of thinking. She shuddered, raking her fingers along the length of his back and feeling the hardness of muscle and sinew under them. More than anything, she wanted to shout out how much she loved him but she held it in.

Ages ago he had told her about a woman he had been seeing, a woman he had almost married whom he had believed was madly in love with him, only to find out that she had been stringing him along. He hadn't given any details and Holly had known not to press. She had kept a steady smile on her face while he had told her this story in passing. Who was she to demand explanations when she, too, had once fancied herself in love, only to realise that once the first flush had faded there was just not enough there to pull them through.

Now, of course, she could see that what she had felt at the time had been nothing. That said, instinct had told her that telling him how much she loved him might not be something he wanted to hear, even though they had now been seeing each other for so long that he must surely guess, just as she did.

He fell back next to her on the sofa and flung his hand over his face before turning on his side and pulling her against him.

'How do you do that?' Luiz murmured. 'How do you always manage to get me so worked up that I can't control myself?' He gave her a crooked smile and outlined her full mouth with his finger. Not only could she get him so worked up that he couldn't control himself, she also managed the impossible feat of making him want to take her all over again within moments of being sated. No woman had ever been able to do that, but then again no woman had ever been so utterly lacking in any kind of agenda. It was just perfect.

'Don't tell me I'm the first to do that.' Holly smiled back at him. She thought of that woman he had once been in love with, the woman she had had no trouble tossing away in a cupboard at the back of her mind. Except now, with a bottle of wine growing steadily warmer outside, and talk of a future between them on the cards, that mysterious woman was demanding some attention. 'What about…you know, Clarissa…the woman you nearly married seven years ago.'

Luiz frowned and drew back to gaze down at her flushed face with a quizzical expression. He had no idea how he had been persuaded into telling her about Clarissa, his biggest mistake and valuable learning curve. But, then again, hadn't he told her a lot of things over time, from that very first moment when he had found himself confiding in her about his father and his feelings of grief that had blinded him to the dangers of the icy country lanes? The grief that had sent his car spinning out of control and landed him in her cottage and, not long after, in her bed. She occupied a special position, one which was far removed from his daily life and, as such, he had ended up telling her a hell of a lot more than he had ever told anyone else in his life.

But now she was smiling and asking about Clarissa and his antenna was picking up signals that were sending little threads of alarm through him. Although he was sure that he was just imagining that. He relaxed and held her close to him.

'Let's not go there.' He nuzzled the column of her neck and felt her shiver responsively. 'The past should never be raked up. What's the point?' He moved to kiss her lips, a long, gentle lingering kiss that did all those wonderfully familiar things to his manhood. 'I don't ask you about your ex,' he pointed out.

'You don't have to.' For once, the feel of him against her and the rub of his arousal pushing to insert itself between her thighs was not enough to bring all her brain functions to a grinding halt. 'You know everything there is to know about him.'

'I don't understand where this is coming from.'

'I'm just curious. What was it about her that you fell in love with?'

Luiz pulled away and lay on his back in silence for a few seconds, hands clasped behind his head. 'It was just one of those relationships that didn't work out,' he said abruptly. 'I should go and have a shower.' He levered himself off the sofa with a twinge of regret. He would have liked to stay put, lost himself in her again, but he really wasn't interested in prolonging a conversation about Clarissa James.

When he had told her about Clarissa, it had been to assuage her curiosity about his unmarried status. Once bitten, twice shy, he had wryly concluded, having omitted most of the details of the relationship—notably the fact that Clarissa James had played him for a fool. He and Clarissa had gone out and she had been a breath of fresh air after his diet of elegant, eligible women. She had been wild, willing and, to start with at least, satisfyingly hard to get. By the time doubts had set in and Luiz had found himself ready to move on, she had declared herself pregnant.

The wild child with the tangle of gypsy-black hair and eccentric clothes that had always looked just right had somehow morphed into a calculating woman who was in a position to call all the shots. It had just been a fortunate accident that he had discovered the stash of contraceptive pills buried in a compartment in her handbag. The packet that was one pill lighter every day for the seven days he had routinely checked.

She had played him for a fool and in the aftermath he had had to endure his family cautioning him about gold-diggers and his sisters gleefully thinking that they could arrange his private life to save him the bother of another mistake—not to mention friends and colleagues to whom he had given no explanation for the break-up, only to say what he had said to Holly, that it hadn't worked out. Doubtless they had drawn other, more elaborate conclusions for the sudden demise of the relationship.

'Why won't you talk about her?' Holly demanded. She sat up and reached down for her discarded underwear. For a few seconds she had the strangest sensation of being suddenly cast adrift on unknown waters. There was an edginess to the atmosphere that made her want just to keep quiet and go with the flow as she had done in the past, but something else was pushing her on to ask him the question that had been playing on her mind for the past couple of months: where were they going? What was the next step for them?

'Because there's nothing to talk about!' Back in his clothes, Luiz turned to see that she had also got into hers although she still had that tousled, thoroughly kissed look that could do things to his body.

'Were you in love with her?'

Luiz paused. He felt as though he had taken a direct hit. The comfortable situation in which she was pleasantly deluded about his wealth, his power and the horror of how it could corrupt no longer felt quite so comfortable. Nor was it so easy to sidestep the reality that the piece of fiction which now lay between them like a gaping chasm wasn't quite as harmless as he conveniently liked to pretend to himself.

'It felt that way at the time,' he grudgingly offered. 'I was wrong.'

'But it left a mark on you.'

'Naturally. That's the thing about bad experiences, they usually do. Now, are we going to spend the rest of the evening sitting here discussing something that's not relevant or are we going to have some of that wine you tell me is waiting outside?'

'It'll be warm.' Suddenly the wine and the crudités seemed a gauche introduction to the serious conversation she had planned. Plus, he just didn't want to talk about Clarissa. He was very forthcoming about his family, about Brazil. He knew so much about so many things that he could debate pretty much anything—he could discuss theatre, opera and art, and he could make her laugh in a thousand ways. If there was ever anything on her mind, anything troubling her, he always knew how to sort it out.

He was physical in ways she could never have imagined and saw nothing wrong in getting his hands dirty helping out at the sanctuary. He listened to everything she said, and she knew that she talked a lot. He probably knew more about her childhood and her background than the friends she had grown up with!

But there were dark areas to him that were practically impenetrable and she had hit one. She knew that even as he turned away and headed out towards the garden where the warm bottle of wine and the crudités, dried at the edges, were waiting for them.

'You're right. It's warm.' He grinned at her and decided that he would put that brief, awkward conversation somewhere safely out of mind. 'Let's scrap the wine and the… eh…sticks of celery and carrot.'

'Crudités,' Holly reluctantly grinned back at him and he gave her a swift hug and dropped a kiss on the corner of her mouth.

'Hmm. If you say so. I've bought you something; you can wear it to go out...' He dipped into his trouser pocket and extracted a small box. The bracelet had cost him thousands. He had chosen it himself. Naturally, he would assure her that it was just a trinket. It was the only way he could give her things and he liked giving her things. Maybe because she never asked for anything. She was neither materialistic, nor was she grasping, but then why would she be when she was clueless as to his financial worth?

'Wow.' The bracelet was studded with what could easily have passed for real diamonds. 'This is amazing, Luiz.' She held it up to the light and watched the way the gemstones caught the rays of the sun. 'You shouldn't have.'

'You say that every time I give you something.'

'Yes, I know. And I keep telling you that there's no need for you to bring me presents all the time. There must be loads of other stuff you need the money for. Living in London isn't cheap...' He had told her that he had a little place in a good enough location. She wasn't entirely sure what 'a good enough location' was and how little his little place might be but, whatever it was and wherever it was located, it would still have cost a lot. Heaven only knew what his mortgage repayments were!

'Let me worry about my finances,' Luiz murmured, urging her back into the house. 'And tell me where you would like to eat.'

'There's something in the oven,' Holly told him breathlessly. Crudités were going to be followed by a casserole. She had followed a recipe. There would be candlelight and she would edge towards the questions she wanted to ask him in stages. She didn't really know why she felt so timid

about discussing their relationship. She just did. It was something he never discussed and his reticence on the subject was
strangely infectious.

'I thought we could eat here…talk a bit.'

'Talk a bit?' Luiz felt a stirring of unease. He had already
diverted an awkward conversation about Clarissa. He hoped
that there were no plans to return to the subject. Walking
into the kitchen a step behind her, he noted that the table had
been elaborately set. Usually, eating in was a casual exercise.
Something quick was rustled up. There always seemed to be
a lot of catching up to do even though he was accustomed
to speaking to her during the week. Food was usually just a
necessary interruption.

'Talk about what?' he demanded.

Holly turned around and gazed at him equably. Underneath the calm exterior, however, she felt unaccountably
nervous, and then for the first time ever a certain amount
of resentment that she should be made to feel nervous about
the prospect of having a perfectly natural conversation with
the man she was in love with.

'Oh, about us.' She gave an unnatural high laugh and
turned away to pour them both a glass of cold wine from
the fridge.

'We talk about us all the time.'

'No, we don't. I mean, we talk about the things we've
been doing during the week, but we don't talk about us.' She
fought past the sinking feeling she was getting at the closed
expression on his face. Her legs felt a little wobbly and she
sat down on the kitchen chair, clutching the wine glass.

'What is there to talk about?' Luiz was deliberately ob-
tuse. The width of the table between them felt like a chasm.
He had become accustomed to her soft, yielding personality. Everything about her was sweetly, generously feminine.
She thought of him in a million little ways and he liked that.

It was why similarly, he put himself out for her like he had never done for any other woman before. Right now, though, he had the disconcerting sensation that she was pulling away from him.

'I've never even seen your place,' Holly told him wistfully.

'You've never asked.' And he had never encouraged. How could he?

'You know everything about me and I know so little about you.'

'You know everything that's of any importance.'

'But you never talk to me about your job—your hopes and dreams for the future.'

'The second I mention the word "computer" you glaze over, Holly. You've been known to state that they're more trouble than they're worth. Why would we waste time discussing them?'

'I'm not saying that we talk about *computers*. I'm saying that you never mention the people you work with. What are they like? Are they fun? I bet the girls in your department are all in love with you...' She laughed but a part of her wondered whether that was really the case. He was so stunning, so charismatic; how could anyone *not* fall in love with him?

'Are you fishing for compliments?' The table between them wasn't a good idea. He needed to be able to touch her. He stood up and pulled a chair towards her so that he could sift his fingers through her long hair. 'You are the only woman on my mind. I wouldn't be able to describe any of the women I see at work, in the street or anywhere else, for that matter.' Nor had he been tempted, once, to stray. Fidelity had never had such a hold over him.

'I think of you all the time.' He gently removed the glass from her hand so that he could tug her towards him and kiss her very gently on her mouth, taking his time. She didn't protest when he undid those wretched buttons, this time not caring whether they ripped or not. This, he thought, was more like it.

*Think of me in terms of what?* Holly wondered. As the woman he enjoyed having sex with? Or as the woman he saw sharing his life with for ever? And, if he thought of sharing his life with her for ever, then how was it that the future had never been a subject for discussion?

'There's no need to feel insecure on that front,' Luiz said huskily. He was getting more aroused by the second. How could she think, even for a minute, that he might look at other women when his responses to her were always so shamefully, glaringly obvious? He pushed her back into the chair and pulled down the top of the dress to look with unashamed, possessive satisfaction at breasts that were flushed from his caresses.

'I don't,' Holly said abruptly. Where was this edgy dissatisfaction coming from? She stood up, roughly buttoned the dress back up and ignored the throbbing between her legs that begged for his fingers, his mouth, the steel-hard length of his erection. 'I know you find me attractive...'

'More than attractive!' He narrowed his eyes on her back. She had turned away from him to begin the process of setting the food out. He wanted to know what she was thinking, although there was a part of him that was getting powerful vibes of discontent. That said, he was certain that he could smooth away all that discontent if only she would allow him. 'You shouldn't have gone to all this trouble.' He stood up, walked towards her and noted her infinitesimal shift away from him. 'Let me help.'

'You can light the candles on the table.' She thought of the crudités shrivelling on the patio outside and the conversation which had yet to get going. At least, get going in the way she had hopefully predicted.

Food on the table, she sat down with lowered eyes. 'I

guess what I'm saying is that we've been an item for well over a year now and I… I think I should be as involved in your life as you are in mine…'

'Are you dissatisfied with the way I treat you?'

'No, of course I'm not, and that's not what I'm saying. You've met all the people who work with me and most of my friends as well. A few weeks ago, I had a party here and invited them all. I haven't met any of yours.' Her hand trembled as she helped herself to some of the casserole which she had spent hours getting just right but which now tasted of cardboard. The candles should have infused the room with a soft, romantic glow. Unfortunately, she felt anything but romantic.

'Everything you're saying points to the fact that you don't think I'm treating you right, whatever you say to the contrary!' Luiz glowered at her down-bent head. Was she determined to wreck the evening? he wondered. 'And yet,' he carried on with remorseless logic, 'Can I remind you that when you developed a food bug after that party I took three days off so that I could stay here and look after you?'

'And I'm really grateful that you did.' The bug had cleared itself out of her system after twenty-four hours and the rest of the time, she wanted to remind him, they had pretty much spent in bed, making love and leaving the running of the sanctuary to Andy and the other helpers. Luiz had had no qualms in announcing her bout of ill health to them and declaring that she would be off work for at least three days.

'And I would do it again!' he stated with an elaborately dismissive gesture designed to imply that he was the sort of big-hearted fellow capable of rising to any occasion. 'Proof enough of your importance in my life. Believe me when I tell you that mopping a woman's brow isn't something I've ever made a habit of!'

Holly allowed herself to relax a little because hearing

that was reassuring. 'It's nice to hear that I'm important to you,' she said softly. 'I know you don't like talking about feelings…I guess a lot of men don't…so it really means a lot for you to say that. Because you're really important to me, Luiz.' She looked across at him with joyous, gleaming eyes. 'The past year and a half has been amazing. I suppose I'm beginning to wonder what the next step is.'

'The next step…?' Luiz felt that his brain was suddenly no longer functioning at its optimum level. His keen mental abilities seemed to have all the agility of a tortoise trudging through treacle.

'The sanctuary runs so well now that, for the first time in ages, I feel I can actually take time off without worrying that something awful might happen in my absence. The accounts are overflowing; there are always animals being rescued, but there's also a long list of people waiting to adopt. I'd really like to see where you live, Luiz, see where you work, meet your friends and maybe…maybe even meet your family. You've told me so much about them, your sisters, your mum… I'd love to see where they live, and for the first time I really think I could take the time off.'

Her smile was beginning to fade at his lack of response. He looked, frankly, shell-shocked. Was she coming on too strong? She knew about his family, their personalities, but she didn't know the details of their lives. Were they poor? He had once told her that there was a great deal of poverty in Brazil. Did he think that she would mind?

'I mean,' she said hurriedly, back-tracking, 'We don't have to just yet. Brazil is an awfully long way away. But I could come down to London…meet some of your friends. I promise not to glaze over if they only want to talk about computers.'

Her voice faltered. Why wasn't he saying anything? Why did he look as though he had been bludgeoned with a sledgehammer? Didn't he realise that this was the normal progression of a relationship? Of course she knew that, after Clarissa, he had not had any meaningful relationships—in fact, from the sounds of it, he had been something of a womanizer—but they had been going out now for well over a year. Surely he must realise that they just couldn't keep drifting? She wasn't getting any younger. Many of her friends were now married; several had started families. Recently, one of the last of her unmarried pals had announced her engagement.

'I just need to know where we're heading,' she said, clearing her throat. 'I just need a sign of commitment.'

# CHAPTER THREE

OF COURSE IT was eventually going to come to this. Luiz could scarcely believe that they had arrived at this cross-roads without him having foreseen the eventuality and taken the necessary precautions. He had never had any intention of indulging in a long-term relationship. He didn't do long-term relationships. But it was all too easy to see now how he had grown lazy after that first, momentous fabrication when he had played fast and loose with the truth of his identity. Without the need to defend himself against a possible gold-digger, he had drifted along and taken what was there for his own enjoyment.

Now her clear blue eyes were anxiously scrutinising his face, waiting for him to say something.

'Why?' Restless energy was pouring through him in disturbing waves and he raked his fingers through his dark hair, his mind travelling down all the angles the conversation could take and crashing into dead ends at each one of them.

'What do you mean *why?*' Holly asked, bewildered because as far as she was concerned she had raised a perfectly reasonable point. 'We've been going out for quite a while. I think I deserve to know where this is heading.' She wished he would stop pacing the room. The giddiness was back, accompanied now by slight feelings of nausea.

'Why does it have to head anywhere?' He paused to stand

in front of her. 'What we have is good. No, it's better than good—it's damn near perfect. Why ruin it with questions about commitment? Why try and box it in and give it a time limit? Who knows what's around the corner?'

'I *know* that,' Holly persevered. 'I *know* there are no guarantees, I *know* that no one knows what's round the corner. But that doesn't mean that I want to continue living in the moment with no thought of the future! I want to know how this is going to *progress* and I don't think I'm being unfair, you know, having this conversation with you. Have I told you that Claire is engaged? Remember Claire—the one with the red hair and the gap between her teeth? You met her at the party...'

'Yes, I remember her.' Loud, extrovert, with a boyfriend who had trailed timidly behind her, fetching drinks and nibbles and making no effort to restrain his girlfriend. Thinking about it, she now struck Luiz as just the sort of subversive woman who would goad Holly into any manner of rebellious thoughts. 'Has she been telling you things? Implying that you can't be happy because there's no diamond ring on your finger? I'm surprised and disappointed that you would allow someone to dictate to you how you should or shouldn't feel!'

'Claire hasn't said anything of the sort to me!' Two bright patches of colour had appeared on her cheeks. One simple question; she had just asked him to clarify where they were going as a couple and he couldn't even bring himself to answer the question directly. Instead, he was happy to imply that she was so stupid and so impressionable that someone else could tell her how she should be feeling!

'Because your friend is engaged doesn't mean that you should be, too.'

'I'm not talking about getting *engaged*...' Although, wasn't it true that ever since their relationship had started she had only seen a future with Luiz in it? She had never daydreamed about a great diamond rock on her finger. But when she thought about the winter coming, and the one after that and the one after that, she had a vision of Luiz right there by her side, helping out as he always did. In her mind, her future was inexorably wrapped up with his and she knew that she had been guilty of assuming that he felt the same way, even if he didn't exactly vocalise it.

'Are you happy with me?' Luiz demanded.

'Of course I am!'

'Then what's the problem?' He felt like someone swimming upstream against a very strong current and he didn't care for the sensation. He liked to be in control. It occurred to him that he had distinctly lacked control when he had allowed this relationship to meander through the weeks and months. He had been instantly attracted to her when she had rescued him after his car crash. He had certainly planned on getting her into bed. He had never played with the possibility that a little time out—a few days of harmless pretence, of letting go of the persona he was compelled to be on a daily basis and all the stresses that came with it—would end up lasting over a year.

The thing to do would be to start thinking clearly and regaining some of that lost control. The obvious solution would be to walk away. He certainly had no intention of encouraging anyone to start thinking in terms of diamond rings, churches and flower girls, however good the sex as between them. No way.

He especially would not be going down that route with a woman who was, frankly, as poor as a church mouse. She might be disingenuous charm itself as long as she believed him to be little more than another one of life's hard workers who saved up to pay the mortgage and grab an annual holiday somewhere cheap and cheerful. But how different would she have been had she known the extent of his wealth?

He had been conned once and he had vowed never to allow that situation to happen again.

Step one in the preventative stakes was to ensure that any lifetime partner—and there certainly wouldn't be one on the horizon in the foreseeable future—would be able to match his wealth. He would only ever marry a woman who didn't have anything to gain in the financial stakes by marrying him.

Holly George was just not suitable. She had raised an issue and the only way to deal with it would be to dispose of her. It sounded heartless, but in the end he would be doing her a favour. If the pot of gold at the end of the rainbow was marriage, then she wasn't going to get the pot of gold from him, and it was kinder to let her go now. When it came to handling the reins of a relationship, *any* relationship, he was the one in control.

Holly turned away and began walking towards the sitting room. Her heart was beating very fast. She just couldn't believe that this conversation was taking place. She had been so secure in their relationship. Had love blinded her to the very real possibility that what he felt for her was nothing more than lust? She couldn't credit that! Lust became eroded over time, lost its urgency… What they had had just got better and better, deeper and deeper, at least as far as she was concerned…

Luiz watched her leave the kitchen and he wanted to throw things, or at the very least haul her back into his arms and make love to her until her questions had been put to rest. He had become accustomed to her smiling, upbeat, eternally optimistic nature. He was used to her glorious, uninhibited chatter. He luxuriated in the company of someone who didn't feel as though she ought to be impressing him. Now, he felt like a monster responsible for draining all the sunshine and light out of her. He had to remind himself that there was nothing he could do to alter the situation and to offer her anything beyond his remit would be to make matters worse in the long run.

'So what are you telling me?' Holly was standing by the bay window, arms folded, every inch of her body radiating tension. 'Are you telling me that what we have isn't going anywhere? Is *never* going to go anywhere? Because if that's the case then I don't see any point to us carrying on. I don't want to be in a relationship where we just drift along until one of us gets bored and decides to call it a day.'

She could hardly breathe. Her chest felt tight. How could he just stand there, looking at her with an inscrutable expression, not saying anything? A treacherous little voice whispered that perhaps she should have left well alone and not said anything, but as soon as the thought flitted through her head Holly knew that she had had to say what was on her mind. She had been feeling strangely emotional over the past few weeks. Holding things in would only exacerbate those heightened emotions.

'Why won't you talk to me, Luiz?' Her eyes brimmed and she chewed her lip in anguish.

'Because you're getting hysterical and you're not saying anything I want to hear.'

'I am *not* getting hysterical! I'm just asking you to tell me how you feel about a future for us.'

'I don't think in terms of future when it comes to my relationships.'

'Because of Clarissa? Is that why?' Holly knew that she was clinging to this as the get-out clause for him. She could deal with him having been hurt in the past and therefore reluctant to commit in the present. That was a situation they could address, one that could be changed. No one could surely allow a past hurt to rule their life for ever? What she found much more difficult to deal with was a blanket refusal to enter the discussion.

Luiz looked at her with veiled eyes. 'Let's not drag history into this, Holly.'

'But you don't understand! I would *never* let you down! You've never told me what happened between the two of you. Maybe if you just opened up on the subject we could work our way through this.'

'I'm not in the mood for psychobabble.'

'So what *are* you in the mood for, Luiz?'

'I wouldn't say no to sliding between the sheets with you…'

'Why does it always have to be about sex?'

'Since when is it always about sex with us?' It was all he wanted from the relationship and yet he was outraged that she should diminish what they enjoyed.

'Well, then, if it's not all about the sex with you, then what else *is* it about?'

Luiz stared at her, speechlessly aware that she had managed to box him in. Since when did any woman think that she had the right to challenge his decisions, ask for clarifications or demand explanations for his behaviour? And yet, he had been with her for an extraordinarily long time. At least, extraordinarily long as far as *he* was concerned. Little by little, he realised that she had made inroads into his levels of tolerance. Somewhere along the line, they had stretched and expanded to accommodate her forthright honesty. That was what now gave her the freedom to stand there, glaring, waiting for him to answer her.

Taking advantage of his temporary silence, Holly thought it a good idea to carry on making her point. There was a certain desperation blossoming inside her but she felt as though if she didn't push as hard as she could beyond that stubborn, autocratic, all-knowing veneer, she would forever rue her hesitation.

'I'm crazy about you. You know that. And if you haven't said so to me in so many words, then…then, you must feel… If it's not just about sex, you must feel…'

In the face of his continuing grim silence, she could feel the confidence leaking out of her. In its place, desperation was giving way to the numbing realisation that perhaps he didn't feel anything for her, or perhaps what he did feel for her just wasn't enough. It wasn't enough to form a basis for a healthy ongoing relationship where holidays were planned and children were discussed and growing old together was a possibility. If all those things had been on the cards, she thought with a sickening jolt, then wouldn't he have suggested her going to Brazil to meet his family? She would have asked him to meet hers ages ago! Had they really been operating on two different planes? Had she been so blind that she hadn't been able to see that what she really wanted was different from what was actually there and, in fact, was leagues apart from what *he* wanted?

Luiz watched as she stammered her way into silence. 'I enjoy your company, Holly, and I care about you.'

'You *care* about me…' Her voice was low and dull. She adored him to distraction and would cheerfully have walked on a bed of burning coals for him. He, on the other hand, *cared* about her. Caring wouldn't go the distance when it came to the bed of burning coals and it wouldn't go the distance when it came to planning for a future.

'Don't knock it.' He read the disappointment on her face but there was no way that he was going to be drawn into offering any more on the subject of how he felt. He could have told her that she turned him on more than any woman ever had, that she had certainly held his attention longer than any woman ever had, but he had a feeling that those sentiments would not have met with an enthusiastic reception.

'I'm not knocking it.' She stumbled over to the sofa, the same sofa where they had made love only a short while ago, and subsided heavily on it. She drew her knees up and wrapped her arms around them.

'Why don't we go outside?' Luiz suggested. Looking at her, he felt uncomfortable in his own skin. 'You told me on the phone that you'd discovered a new walk.' She enjoyed the great outdoors. A little bit of fresh air might calm her frayed nerves. He found himself giving her a last chance to climb back from her inappropriate meltdown and he was half-angry at his leniency.

'I'm not really in the mood to go walking.' Her voice was barely audible.

'Well, sitting there sulking isn't going to solve anything.'

'I thought I meant more to you.'

Luiz sighed and joined her on the sofa. He had to restrain himself from touching her. It was something he badly wanted to do. 'I could tell you that you mean a lot to me, but the follow-on isn't that we're going to get engaged like your friend. The next chapter in our story isn't going to be marriage. I'm very sorry, Holly, but the next chapter in our story is *never* going to be marriage.'

'I'm not talking about marriage.'

'Of course you are.' He had deliberately blinded himself to the fact that she was a romantic. She might work hard in the sanctuary, as hard as any man would in similar circumstances, but that didn't mean that she didn't like the picnics in summer, or get teary-eyed during sentimental movies, or lose herself in ridiculous love stories. Now, he thought with regret, was the time to be brutal.

'You could never tolerate anything less than full commitment and that will not be happening, at least not with me. I should have made myself clearer on the subject from the beginning. I didn't and I am to blame for that.' He wished she would make eye contact but she was staring straight ahead and her body was as stiff as a plank of wood. 'Trust me when I tell you that you're better off without me,' Luiz said truthfully, and she looked at him with incredulity.

'How can you say that? That's the sort of thing men say when they can't face having an honest conversation—*you're better off without me, I need a little space.* That's what men say when they're about to walk out and they're clearing it with their conscience. I've read hundreds of articles on that subject!'

Luiz fought against smiling. She loved reading self-help books and anything to do with emotions and psychology. She had a tendency to answer any quiz in any magazine. Occasionally she had forced him into taking part and then analysed his answers so that she could inform him of the person he was. There was no getting away from the fact that he would miss things like that.

'There are things about me you don't know, Holly.' Luiz hadn't really considered the possibility of coming clean with her. What would be the point when it wouldn't change anything? But he now felt that he owed it to her. There was no moral integrity in exiting this relationship in a welter of half-truths. If he did that, he knew that he would, one day, regret the omissions.

'All that business with your ex… I know it's not my fault that you won't discuss any of it with me…' He must have really loved her, Holly was thinking glumly. She had taken the best of him and had made sure that he would have nothing left to give another woman.

'Partly.'

Holly barely took that in. She was busily thinking about the bottle of wine growing warmer and warmer outside, along with the shrivelled crudités and the dried-up cheese savouries, all part of her plan to coax him into something he was incapable of giving her. In her mind, she was trying to imagine what life was going to be like if this turned out to be the last time she saw him and she couldn't get her head round that. She wanted to fling herself at him and tell him that she loved him enough for the two of them.

'I want you to look at me.'

'What for? What difference does it make?' But she shifted until she was facing him and he was so close to her that she could just reach out and run her fingers through his dark hair.

'Prepare to be shocked. Clarissa wasn't, as you seem to imagine, the love of my life.'

'She wasn't?' Holly's heart lifted. 'I thought you didn't want to talk about her because you were still in love with her and the memory hurt too much.'

'I don't talk about her because she turned out to be a lying, scheming bitch.'

'Oh.' Holly was now fully invested in whatever Luiz had to say. In fact, she had completely forgotten her woeful projections of life without him in it. Whatever he had to say to her, she knew that the an unforgettable ex was one difficulty removed from the equation and that could only be a good thing. 'What do you mean?' She couldn't resist extending her hand and running it gently along his arm. She could feel bunched muscle and it sent a pleasurable shiver through her.

'You might not want to do that…' Luiz's jaw tensed and he vaulted upright. The effect of her soft hand on his arm was as dramatic as a white-hot branding iron. He put some distance between them, moving to sit on a chair.

'Do what?'

'Touch me. You touch me and I can't help but touch you back.'

'You have my permission.' Holly thought that he might

not want to promise her anything beyond today, but she still had a huge amount of power over him. Couldn't she use that power to make small inroads into that tough fortress he insisted on building around himself to protect his emotions? Maybe it wasn't the 'all or nothing' scenario she had painted. Life wasn't black and white. It was always full of grey areas…

'You wanted to talk. We'll talk.'

'We can talk and touch at the same time.'

Luiz stifled a groan. His fabled and formidable self-control, on which his empire was built and which had always stood him in good stead when it came to women, was missing in action. But wasn't it always when it came to Holly? With her, he had never had to use it and lack of use had made it rusty. Her invitation to touch was almost more than he could bear.

'Fifteen minutes ago you were going to chuck me out because I wasn't going to propose,' he said grittily. Holly smiled sheepishly at him and reddened.

'I was emotional. I've been a little emotional recently. I don't know why. Maybe it's because all my friends seem to be settling down. Maybe I feel like time is racing by. It all seemed to build up inside me. You were…um…telling me about Clarissa…'

Luiz cursed himself for being tempted to accept her explanation and run with it. The promise of the status quo being re-established dangled in front of him, as tantalising as a banquet to a starving man. No more talk of commitment. Back to him having her here, the one window in his life where there was no stress…

He savagely culled the alluring image before it could truly take hold and make him lose sight of the fact that this was not a situation destined to go away. Holly might be prepared to back away from the gauntlet she had foolishly laid down, but the gauntlet would still be there and it would only be a question of time before the inevitable happened. But, hell, she sat there on the couch with her fair hair spilling all over the place and her big blue eyes staring at him, her mouth half-open, as though on the brink of voicing a thought… He had to grit his teeth and push ahead.

'Clarissa thought that I could be her ticket to the good life.' He dragged his eyes away from the soft fullness of her lips which mirrored the exquisite abundance of her breasts. Just thinking about touching them again was enough to make him lose focus. On top of all the reasons why this relationship was a poor idea, he ruthlessly added *'unacceptable loss of self-control'* to the list.

'It's understandable,' Holly conceded reluctantly. 'I guess that doesn't make her much different from me…'

'You're not understanding.' He stood up, raked his fingers through his hair and sat back down. Every nuance of expression and every slight movement of his body spoke tellingly of a level of awkward restlessness which was completely alien to the Luiz Gomez Holly knew and loved. While a part of her wanted to jump to her feet, hold him tight and apologise for ever mentioning anything, another part of her was already uneasily accepting that she had started something from which there was no retreat.

Luiz prowled the room before settling for a spot by the bay window and leaning against it.

The fading sun poured through the glass behind him and threw him into shadow. Now, she couldn't see the expression on his face at all.

'Clarissa saw me as a passport to the sort of lifestyle she could only dream of.' He could tell from her silence that she was confused, didn't have a clue what he was talking about. 'She wanted me for my money, Holly, and she would have done everything within her power to get what she wanted, including faking a pregnancy.'

'I'm not following you. What money? What are you talking about?' Holly felt as though she had stepped into a parallel universe, one in which everything looked the same, sounded the same, but was somehow completely different, altered and reconfigured into the unrecognisable. The Luiz talking to her in that flat, impersonal voice wasn't *her* Luiz. She sensed that on a subconscious level and it made her pulses race with sudden, gripping apprehension.

'Tell me who you think I am.'

'You're Luiz Gomez. You work as a salesman. Computers... Why would anyone think that you could be a passport to...to...? How much do salesmen get *paid,* for goodness' sake?'

'My name isn't Luiz Gomez.'

'I'm sorry?' Holly could only stare. She half-stood up, mouth agape, wondering if she had heard correctly. 'If you're not Luiz Gomez, then who the heck *are* you?'

'Sit down, Holly!' He barely had time to make it across the room and catch her before she hit the ground.

Holly came to quickly, but it took her a few seconds to reorient and when she did his words came rushing back at her in a poisonous flood that threatened to make her black out again. She squirmed away from him, eyes wide with horror and incomprehension.

'What are you talking about? Don't come near me! Who *are* you?'

'I'm going to get you a glass of brandy. It'll calm you down.'

'I don't want any brandy. I just want you to tell me what's going on!'

'I'm not a travelling salesman, selling computers and saving up to buy a house. My name isn't Gomez, my name is Casella—Luiz Casella—and I'm worth more than most people can only dream about. Clarissa wanted the lifestyle I could give her. She faked a pregnancy to rope me into marriage, the plan being that she would suffer a "miscarriage" shortly after the wedding. I finally and completely opened my eyes to the level to which people will sink in an effort to secure financial security. I understood once and for all the concept of gold-diggers.

'I made up my mind on the spot that, if the consequence of taking a chance on a relationship might result in another Clarissa moment, then no relationship with its promises of happy-ever-after would be worth it. And if I ever *were* to go for the long-term choice, then I would do so with a woman of independent means, someone to whom my money would be an irrelevance. It would be a marriage of mutual convenience. I have neither the time nor the inclination for emotional risk-taking.'

Holly heard what he was saying but was suffering from information overload. Her mind had stuck on the very first revelation that he wasn't who he said he was.

'But *why?* You lied. I don't get it.'

Luiz could feel her withdrawal from him. He could detect that light in her eyes that spoke of suspicion and mistrust. She hadn't yet reached the point of anger and bitterness, but those two emotions would come and he had to remind himself that life was a cruel place and being toughened up by unpleasant, unexpected situations was always, in retrospect, character building.

Right now, though… He flushed darkly and flung his arms out in an exotically foreign gesture.

'Why would you *lie* to me? How could you *do* that? I helped you and you…you *lied* to me about who you were and I just don't understand that! I don't get it.'

'Then you haven't been listening.'

'And you can stop treating me like an idiot, Luiz! Or are you lying about that as well? Is Luiz *really* your first name or will you come clean about that in a little while? Will you tell me that you're actually called Richard, or—or Tom, or Fred? And that you're not really from Brazil at all? You're from East London and your father worked on a market stall!'

'You're upset. I understand.'

'How can you tell me that you've spent the last year and a half lying to me and be so…so *calm?*' She knew why. It was because she had fallen head over heels in love with a man whose core was a block of ice.

'Would you like to listen to what I have to say or would you rather I leave?'

Faced with that stark choice, Holly bit back the onset of tears gathering pace and remained silent. She was numb all over. 'I want to know why. I deserve to know.'

'When I crashed my car…'

'The car you couldn't even be bothered to recover. You didn't even go through the insurance company to see what money you could get back… I should have twigged that normal people don't write off cars just like that. It wasn't some old banger, was it?'

'No. No matter. It was still disposable.'

Like a computer, suddenly rebooted and finally working to full capacity, Holly was adding up all the things that should have tallied and opened her eyes to a man who wasn't just an ordinary Joe Bloggs. His casual way with money; the ease with which he accepted subservience as his due; his in-built self-assurance; his assumptions that he was always right…

'When I crashed and you rescued me, I wasn't in a particularly good place. I had just closed a deal in Durham and was on my way back to London. I came here and in a split second I made the decision that it would be an idea to take time out from being a Casella. Chances are you wouldn't have heard of me anyway, but there was a chance that you might. The Durham deal was all over the newspapers. I never foresaw that we would still be in a relationship a year and a half later.'

'But why wouldn't you have wanted me to know your real name? Why would you think that it would have made a difference knowing who you were and…and…?'

'Experience has taught me that people are rarely open and spontaneous when they know the extent of my wealth. They pander, they fawn, they even fake pregnancy… It's just the way it is.'

Holly's sluggish brain was reaching its inexorable conclusions and she was dismayed, hurt and horrified. The man she loved was rich. She didn't know *how* rich, but if he could dismissively shrug off the loss of an expensive car without a backward glance, then *very*. Clarissa had hunted him down and tried to trap him because of his money. No doubt he was right when he told her that people adapted to please him.

But how could he ever have thought that she would be one of those people? Because he was suspicious. Whilst she had thrown herself into an open and honest relationship, there had been a part of him always holding back, always keeping her at arm's length.

'Did you think that I would be after your money if I had known that you were rich?'

'I knew that the thought of not having to wonder whether you were was a very liberating experience.'

'You haven't answered my question.'

'I'm not a man who takes chances,' was the extent of his explanation, but it was enough for Holly to sag like a broken doll.

Luiz savagely told himself that this was just one very good reason why it paid to steer clear of emotional involvements.

He had told her the truth. He didn't now want hours of tearful post mortems, but neither could he make himself stand up and head for the door, and that paralysis enraged him.

'So all this time…' She looked at him wonderingly, still feeling as though she was in a nightmare, one from which she might awaken any time even though the still-thinking part of her had already accepted that this was no bad dream. 'You've been using me like a plaything. A bit of light relief on the weekends. You come here, there are no demands made on you, you help out at the sanctuary and then you leave and return to your real life. Are there other women out there? In your real life?'

'This is ridiculous.' Luiz stood up and looked down at her vulnerable fair head. He cursed himself for having landed up in this situation but refused to ask himself if he would have walked away from it, had he had a crystal ball that first time he had met her. He shoved his hands in his pockets as the silence thickened around them, heavy with accusation.

'Don't bother to answer that,' Holly muttered thickly. 'I don't think I want to know the answer.'

Luiz hesitated as pride warred with some other emotion he couldn't quite identify but which he summed up as normal human decency. 'Of course there were no other women,' he imparted in a driven undertone. 'When I am with a woman, I don't stray.'

'Except you make sure that none of them outstay their welcome. You wouldn't want any of them to get ideas above their station!'

'Sarcasm doesn't suit you.'

'I didn't think I was being sarcastic. I thought I was being realistic. Because, *realistically,* you'll never have a committed relationship with anyone you think might be after your money. *Like me.* Will you?'

'This discussion is running out of steam,' Luiz said coldly.

'I apologise for having misled you but I do not apologise for now telling you the lie of the land.'

'All that stuff you gave me…' Holly fingered the 'fake' ruby.

'None of the jewellery was paste.' Luiz watched as it dawned on her how much money was stashed away in various parts of the cottage, because she didn't own a jewellery box. 'I make a generous lover. In this instance, it was a luxury I wasn't allowed.'

'Is that how you've always treated the women you've gone out with? You buy them stuff and then dump them before they can get too clingy?' She laughed shortly. 'I can understand why you must have enjoyed the novelty of sleeping with a woman who didn't know who you really were.'

'Who wasn't aware of my real name or my position,' Luiz corrected.

'Whatever.' In the space of a few hours, Holly felt as though she had aged ten years. Gone was the hopeful enthusiasm and the absolute certainty that she had met her soul mate and was destined to spend the rest of her life with him. She looked at him expressionlessly. 'I think it's time you left now.'

Drained of all emotion, she could only watch as he gave a slight nod. Nor did she get up as he gathered his things, pausing only to glance at her over his shoulder, one hand on the door, a man now ready to take his leave. She knew he must have telephoned a taxi and she also knew that he would be in the hall waiting for it to arrive. She was keeping it together but she knew that, when that front door clicked shut behind him, she would no longer be able to contain the anguish.

# CHAPTER FOUR

'YOU'RE NOT FOOLING anyone, Hols. You smile a lot but, just between you and me, you're letting yourself go...' Andy, who still managed to look dapper in muddy, low-slung jeans and his close-fitted knitted jumper, was standing back and looking at her with a critical eye. 'Frankly you're putting on weight.'

'I've been comfort eating...a little,' Holly confessed defensively. 'It's getting colder, salads don't work in October. Besides, what's the point of growing all those vegetables if I don't eat them? And I have to have *something* to eat with them.' But it was a paltry excuse. She *had* put on weight in the nine weeks since Luiz had walked out of her house. She was shamelessly indulging her sweet tooth and finding it hard to care if she gained a pound or two.

It was just her luck that Andy was proudly gay and into anything and everything to do with fashion, despite the fact that he worked in a job that came with mud as part of the package. He never failed to let her know that his jaundiced eyes were noticing each creeping pound she put on.

Ever since Luiz had left, Andy had seen it as his mission to 'get her out of herself.' He delivered lectures on the importance of learning curves, arranged parties to which he invited single straight friends and watched beadily from the sidelines as she steadfastly failed to notice any of them.

'You need to move on,' he now said kindly. 'That sexy hunk of yours won't be back and it's no good eating your way through the biscuit tin while you wait in vain.'

'I'm not *eating my way through the biscuit tin* and I'm not *waiting in vain, either...*' But she smiled reluctantly and nodded when he invited her yet again to another of his parties, this one a soiree where she would be able to meet a couple of really nice guys into music: very hip, very cool, although he could try for an accountant if asked nicely...

So far, he had introduced her to a doctor, a hairdresser, several artists and two farmers, both of whom she had gone to school with and neither of whom elicited anything other than polite enquiries about their parents. He was determined to stop her from brooding, and she was grateful, just as she was grateful to all her friends who had rallied round and were equally determined to make her forget the whole Luiz episode and treat it as though it had never happened.

Holly knew that they were right. She needed to move on. She hadn't heard a word from Luiz since he had walked out of her life. Several times she had been tempted to call his mobile just to hear the sound of his rich drawl, and she had had to fight the urge with all her might.

Now, more than ever, she was alert to the reality that time was not standing still. While she succumbed to fudge cake and hearty pasta meals, Luiz had well and truly forgotten about her.

'He's found someone else,' she blurted out as they closed the final gate on a donkey that had come to the sanctuary after the death of his owner, and began walking up to one of the outbuildings which had been converted into a comfortable changing room.

Her shoulders were hunched and she kept her eyes firmly on the ground. 'I looked on the Internet...just a peep to see what was happening with him. I know I shouldn't have. Curiosity killed the cat and all that.'

'Well, I'm surprised it took him that long,' Andy said acerbically. 'The man has a reputation. I've done a bit of reading up on him myself. If you were over him, you wouldn't be checking to see what he was up to,' he belatedly admonished and Holly cast him a sheepish, sidelong glance.

'You should see her.' She hovered miserably by the door to the changing rooms, which was one of the upgrades covered by the so-called money that had been lying around in an account after the sale of the farm but which Holly now suspected had just been money donated by Luiz to cover the cost of sex with the woman he'd had no intention of settling down with. There were two shower cubicles, toilets and sinks on either side, one for the men and the other for the women; the black-and-white tiled floor, always scrupulously clean, was rescued from appearing too clinical by the addition of a couple of chairs and a small table. Leading off from the changing area, a comfortable room was big enough to cater for everyone at mealtimes when the weather was foul and they wanted to escape from the great outdoors.

'Don't think about that,' Andy urged.

'She's beautiful. I mean *really* beautiful. Plus she's Brazilian, from a very important, very rich family. And she's skinny and tall. She's the exact opposite of me. There's loads of speculation that they're going to be married.'

She could have elaborated on the slew of pictures she had pored over the evening before. Luiz and Cecelia Follone laughing as they stepped out of a limo for the premiere of a movie; snapped unawares leaving a restaurant; posing in front of the theatre. They had only been seeing each other for three weeks, yet he seemed as comfortable standing next to her as though they had been going out for centuries.

Holly had spent a sleepless night torturing herself with

the thought that he was over the moon at having had a lucky escape from a country bumpkin living in the back of beyond, someone who had yet to discover the joys of shopping, who seldom wore make-up and who, as far as he was concerned, had been a potential gold-digger only saved from revealing her baser instincts because he had lied to her about the scale of his wealth.

Andy was right, she thought later. It was time to be proactive and to move on. She would try and show a healthy interest in the musicians. She would definitely go on a crash diet. In no time at all, she would be thin and her life would be back on track…

In his towering office in the city, Luiz had swivelled his chair away from his desk and was absently gazing out to a view of a city always on the move. In one hand he idly played with some of the bits of jewellery he had given to Holly over the time they had been lovers. She had returned the lot to him weeks ago and for some reason he had kept the stuff shoved at the back of his desk drawer.

It was grey and miserable outside, which meant that Cecelia would be complaining. She complained a lot, and she loathed the English weather, which she claimed to be depressing and responsible for her scrupulously maintained tan fading faster than normal. Right now, she would be complaining to Ana, her maid, who had travelled over with her.

Tonight he would be taking her to the opera. The thought of it induced a feeling of inertia which he knew was not in keeping with a man supposedly in the throes of a relationship. An extremely suitable relationship. He had met her through a friend of his mother's and Cecelia's aunt, who had looked him up on the spur of the moment with her niece in tow.

Privately Luiz thought that she had wanted to offload her high-maintenance niece and she had caught him just at the precise moment in time when he had been contemplating his recent loss of libido with vast annoyance, wondering whether he shouldn't be thinking about settling down and forgoing a continuing lifestyle of interchangeable airheads.

As yet, Cecelia had still to fire his libido, but he was certain that the lack of sexual chemistry was a temporary drawback. He had been working ungodly hours since Holly had disappeared from his life and lack of sleep could do all sorts of things to a person's body. The fact remained that Cecelia was perfect for him. Any union between them could only be to his advantage. Her family was on a par with his, from the point of view of wealth. Like most pampered women, she was far more interested in the business of building up and maintaining an enviable social circle than she was in spending quality time with him. She enjoyed being seen with the right people in the right places. She was not the type to start making demands about the amount of time he devoted to work. It was all to the good.

As he thought about her, he ran his fingers over the smooth stones on the bracelets and rings that had been returned to him without even the courtesy of a note.

Immediately, the image of a leggy, Brazilian brunette was overlaid by the image of a small, curvaceous blonde who probably didn't know a manicure from a pedicure and had most likely never stepped foot in a spa to get any of the treatments that Cecelia did on a more or less daily basis.

Luiz's lips thinned. He loathed it when he was distracted by the memory of Holly and it was a distraction that occurred far too frequently for his liking. Supposedly this was because, for the first time in his life, *he* had not been the one to terminate the relationship. Naturally the way it had ended would have left a sour taste in his mouth. Naturally, she would crop up in his thoughts more than he wanted. Obviously, this was an occurrence that would disappear soon enough, but in case it didn't…

Luiz glanced down at his mobile phone and scrolled to the text message which he had received the evening before. It was brief: she wanted to meet him. He had no idea why and he had seriously been tempted to press the delete button without bothering to reply. But then he had been struck by the thought that seeing her might just put paid to her annoying and lingering presence at the back of his mind. He would be reminded that she had been little more than an unusual distraction. He would stop thinking about her and sex in the same breath and gain some much-needed perspective on a slice of his life that he was glad to be rid of.

He allowed himself the luxury of wondering what would be bringing her to London; naturally, he had informed her in a text as brief as hers had been that, whilst he would grant her an audience, he certainly wouldn't be doing so up north. If she wanted to see him that badly, then she would have to do the unthinkable and travel south.

He couldn't imagine what would possess her to get in touch with him after all this time. Had she begun to regret her hasty departure from his life? She had returned all the priceless jewellery. Maybe she had started thinking that that had been a wrong move, bearing in mind how much money she would have been able to get had she decided to sell them.

In the end, people were always motivated by money. It was a disappointing truth. He was in no doubt that, under the waffle she would have prepared, she would be on a begging mission. Maybe something had collapsed in the animal shelter, or the dodgy plumbing in the cottage needed replacing. Not to beat about the bush, one of a dozen things could have happened that required financial input and doubtless she had reached the conclusion that he was the best source of money she had.

It would definitely be satisfying to watch her squirm. Any lingering nostalgia he had would be wiped out the second she lowered her eyes, cleared her throat and asked if he could lend her just enough money to…do whatever she needed it to do. He would think with warmth and relief then of Cecelia and the fact that she would never need to ask him for money.

A cynical smile curved his sensuous mouth. He decided that this unexpected visit from Holly was just the thing. In fact, he couldn't wait…

Dithering outside the most impressive office building she had ever seen, all smoked glass and metal, Holly chewed her lip and clutched her backpack in front of her like a talisman. People swerved around her, coming and going. They all wore dark business suits and carried briefcases or computer bags slung over their shoulders. These were people in a hurry and on a mission. When she had sent that text to Luiz, asking to meet up, she had expected him to suggest somewhere neutral, maybe a restaurant or a coffee bar. The fact that he couldn't even be bothered to leave his office to see her was a stark reminder of how little she meant to him and how thoroughly she had been forgotten. He was quite literally prepared to 'grant her an audience' between emails.

She knew she should be neither hurt nor surprised by that. She had invested far more in their relationship than he had. He wasn't going to be eager to see her and he wouldn't be interested in catching up. In fact, she was slightly surprised that he had agreed to see her at all. She glumly thought that, by the time she was finished saying what she had to say, he would be heartily wishing that he had refused.

Taking a deep breath, she forged a way through the busy swarm of people, either leaving for or returning from lunch.

In her shapeless, long-sleeved dress and her thin waterproof anorak, she felt as conspicuous as an elephant at a tea party. She knew, as she was propelled through the revolving doors and ejected like a sack of potatoes into the vast, opulent foyer of the building he had directed her to, that people were staring at her. Politely staring; wondering what on earth she was doing there. She knew that if she didn't act purposefully right now that a security guard would materialise and offer to show her out of the building. There would be an implicit threat that the police would be involved if she didn't go quietly.

How on earth had it come to this? It was the question she had been asking herself for the past week. She had made the appointment to see her doctor, as she had been feeling under the weather recently. A prescription and maybe a pep talk on the curative aspect of time had been the only things she'd expected...

Someone bumped into her from behind, a young girl in a snappy black suit carrying the obligatory briefcase and Holly mumbled an awkward apology and was rewarded with a gimlet stare and raised eyebrows.

Her frayed nerves were well and truly reduced to rubble at this timely reminder of how out of place she was here and how horrendous and awkward the next half an hour was going to be.

Indeed, her thoughts were in such a state of meltdown that she was barely aware of the next ten minutes or so, during which a friendly girl, one of four positioned behind a circular desk, pointed to where she should sit whilst one of Luiz's secretaries came for her. Then, ten minutes later, she was herded off to a private lift and whooshed upwards so that her already sick and nervous stomach churned even more sickly and nervously.

She ceased noticing the curious stares as she was ushered into a huge space that smelled of money being made and deals being done. She paid absolutely no attention to the opulence of her surroundings. She no longer felt insignificant next to the thirty-something-year-old clones with their ears pressed to phones and their fingers tapping on computer keyboards, their body language proclaiming that they couldn't stop because they were in the middle of making huge profits for their company.

She blindly followed the middle-aged woman in front of her while every fear and apprehension she had nurtured on the train down coalesced into a sickening knot in the pit of her stomach.

She desperately wanted to reach out, grab the woman by the hand and tell her that she had made a terrible mistake; could she please just leave now? But, before she could open her mouth to utter a word, they were at the end of the corridor where she was staring into a boardroom, then turning left through a suite, then an office, then facing a heavy door which was very firmly closed.

Holly felt as though she had had no time to register this side of a Luiz she'd never known existed, no chance to appreciate the world he worked in. She felt that she should have paid more attention to her surroundings. It would have given her the opportunity to stoke up the old anger and fan the flames of hurt and disillusionment which she would need to see her through the next half an hour.

She felt vulnerable, under-prepared and scared to death as the heavy door was pushed open. Her first glimpse of Luiz after all these weeks was of his back, turned away from her as he stared through an impressive bank of windows overlooking the city.

Luiz was aware of his secretary showing Holly in but he only turned around when he heard the soft click of the door being shut. Still playing with the bits of jewellery she had returned to him, he now dropped them into the depths of his trouser pocket and looked at his visitor with a cool, unreadable expression, his antennae on full alert as he studied her, taking in every detail of her appearance.

She had put on weight. Or had she? He couldn't tell because for the past few weeks the women with whom he had come into contact had all been thin and lanky. Next to any of them someone with even the merest hint of a curve would appear overweight. Next to her, Cecelia was a stick insect.

Familiarity kicked in. The memory of her voluptuous, sexy body slammed into him with the unexpected force of a freight train. He was angrily aware of his dormant libido gathering force and breaking through the barrier of indifference he was keen to keep in place, even though she couldn't have been dressed in a less flattering outfit. Having not seen him for over two months, she couldn't even be bothered to dress for the occasion! He thought that she could have tried a bit harder to impress, for someone on a begging mission.

'I can't spare you a lot of time,' he said, moving to sit and watching intently as she hesitantly remained where she was, as though ready to take flight at a moment's notice. He was riveted by the untouched prettiness of her face. He had contrived to forget the appeal her lack of artifice had always held for him, but he was fast realising that the memory of that had been buried in a very shallow grave indeed. The hope that Cecelia might benefit from comparison wasn't happening. In fact, it was a struggle to revive the image of the Brazilian beauty with her full, pouting mouth and model size-zero figure.

'That's okay.' In her peripheral vision, Holly was conscious of a comfortable leather sofa against a stark white wall on which hung an imposing abstract painting in bold colours. On the opposite side, a slightly smaller desk was backed by bookshelves, all high-gloss white. But really her eyes were glued to Luiz, as imposing, impressive and sinfully good-looking as he had been in her head, where he had continued to plague her waking moments and invade her thoughts when she was asleep at night.

'So…what can I do for you?' He tapped his pen restively on the surface of his desk and lounged back in the chair. Keen eyes noted the slow crawl of colour into her cheeks, confirming his suspicion that her visit was financially motivated. Naturally, he wanted to wait until she was forced to confess the reason for her visit. There was already a cynical twist to his mouth in anticipation of the predictable denouement of her presence in his office but, when the silence stretched on and on, he finally clicked his tongue impatiently and leant forward.

'You were never short of something to say, Holly, so why the dumbstruck silence?'

'I…I'm not sure where to begin…' Her voice sounded unnaturally high and tinged with guilt. She hadn't expected to be thrown in at the deep end, made to feel unwelcome, granted none of the usual pleasantries that might have put her a little more at ease. He acted as though *she* had been the one to blame for the break-up of their relationship! As though *he* hadn't been the guilty party…the man who had lied to her and led her up the garden path!

Hard on the heels of that thought came the realisation that he could behave however he chose because in his head he was probably guilty of nothing. So he had lied to her, but he certainly wouldn't feel mortified at that because to feel mortified, he would also have had to care about her and he hadn't. That was the bottom line. Her soft mouth firmed.

'Shall I give you a helping hand?' Luiz queried in a silky-smooth voice that somehow managed to get her back up and reduce her already scattered ability to think even more.

'How could you do that? You don't know what I've come here to say,' Holly intoned in a nervous whisper.

'I can take a guess…'

'How?' Confusion tore into her as she tried to fathom out how he could possibly suspect the reason for her visit. Was he a mind reader? He had always been spectacularly good at placing her moods and had always seemed to instinctively know what she was about to say. Plus, she *had* gained weight. All over there was just…more of her. She had gone up a bra size, and that was underestimating things. Self-consciously, she felt her breasts tighten and she shifted a little. For a man who could take in every detail of a woman's body in seconds, he would have spotted that in a flash. She thought that it might make her job a little easier if she didn't have to spell it all out in black and white. Caving in to his superior knowledge, and not doubting for a second that he had guessed why she was there, Holly sagged. 'I suppose it's pretty obvious.'

'It is to me. For God's sake, Holly, why don't you take that ridiculous jacket off and sit?'

'You don't have much time. I wouldn't want to impose… I just wanted to say what I have to say…leave you to mull it over…' But she awkwardly removed the anorak and slunk into the chair opposite his desk.

Luiz gave a sharp intake of breath. He would have had to be blind not to see how those luscious curves were even more tempting now. Her generous breasts were more than evident underneath the baggy dress. His jaw hardened as he fought to contain a crazy urge to lock the office door and discover for himself just how voluptuous she was underneath the unappealing clothing.

'What's there to mull over?' he demanded harshly. 'Just tell me what you need the money for. What's gone wrong at the sanctuary? High winds wrecked some of the enclosures? Or is it the cottage? That damn building's so ancient that you might as well resign yourself to the uphill task of finding money to fix things forever more until you decide to sell it.' He reached into the desk drawer and pulled out a cheque book. 'For old times' sake, I'll give you however much you want, but after this the well is dry…'

Holly looked at him in a daze, not quite following what he was saying to her.

'You think that I've come for *money?*' Yet why was she so shocked and hurt? Hadn't he told her weeks ago, when they had parted company, that in his eyes all women were gold-diggers unless their fortunes could match his? Including her? Was it any wonder that he was looking at her now, ill-dressed and nervous, and jumping to all the wrong conclusions?

'What else?'

'You really *are* the most cynical person I've ever met, Luiz. I don't suppose I would have liked you at all if I had met…the guy sitting in front of me right now, waving a cheque book around and asking me how much money I had come for. When we were together, you never behaved like an arrogant bore who thought that he could throw money around and get whatever he wanted.'

Luiz flushed darkly, caught off-guard by the pained bitterness in her voice. He leaned back and folded his hands behind his head. If she wanted to get to her point via a circuitous route, then he would let her but, the 'arrogant bore' label rankled.

'But the arrogant bore sitting in front of you is the guy I really am,' he murmured smoothly.

'You were never arrogant when you were with me,' Holly said in a strained voice.

'But then, I was Luiz Gomez when I was with you. Here I am Luiz Casella, and I don't have time to go round the houses with you, so why don't you tell me what you're doing here and have done with it?' *Arrogant bore*... More than anything, he loathed the disappointment and pity in her face when she had said that. When he had walked out, he had left her angry and hurt. Now, surrounded by the trappings of his vast empire, she wasn't impressed, she was disenchanted. Wealth didn't seem to make him more of a man in her eyes.

Nerves making her fidgety, Holly glanced away and said abruptly, 'I read somewhere that you're going out with... someone now.'

Luiz's immediate thought was to ask whether she was jealous...jealous enough to trek all the way down to London to confirm a rumour...jealous enough to realise that she had lost a good thing, whatever her high-minded reasons might have been at the time.

'Where did you read that?' he asked.

'On the Internet.' Holly blushed at the admission.

'Really? I'm surprised that you were interested enough to try and check me out.' But he had to admit that it gave him a kick to think that she had been.

'I wanted to find out who the person I'd been seeing for the past year and a half really was,' she said defensively. 'You're famous.'

'I've acquired some standing in the business community.'

'I felt like I was reading about someone I didn't know. You own properties all over the world; your have companies and businesses all over the world. What on earth did you ever see in me? Didn't I bore you to death?'

'You were...'

'A novelty,' Holly bitterly filled in the blanks. 'A change of scene—and a change is as good as a rest, isn't it? And your usual scene when it comes to women are glamorous models and celebrities. There were reports and pictures about the new woman in your life...Cecelia Follone. I guess she's the sort of woman you described as your ideal long-term partner…the right background…the right *look*.'

'And that's why you came here? To find out whether there was any truth behind the rumours?' He had temporarily forgotten about Cecelia and didn't care for the reminder that she was supposed to be his 'ideal long-term partner'.

'No,' Holly said quietly. 'I'm sure there's a lot of truth behind the rumours. And I haven't come here because I care. I don't. The Luiz I cared about and fell in love with disappeared and was replaced by a Luiz I don't know.'

And yet, even as the words poured out, she was drawn and shaken by the fierce tug of familiarity, of somehow *knowing* that, underneath the polished surface veneer, there would surely be the person she had grown to know. She shoved aside the wimpish, craven urge to see the three-dimensional man, to marry the two sides of the coin, and instead reminded herself of the undeserved suspicions he had levelled against her. The distrust that had shaken her belief in him, the ease with which he had written her off as a potential opportunist when, after all the time they had spent together, he should have known that he was miles out in his assumptions.

'Your somebody else,' she said, drawing in a deep breath. 'Do you love her?'

'Come again?'

'The girl you're going out with…do you love her?'

'That question is inappropriate.' He glanced pointedly at his watch. Every single thing she had said since she had walked into his office had offended him. He was savagely aware that, while her very presence should repel him, he still couldn't prevent himself from responding to her with a physical reaction that seemed to be utterly out of his control. He was riveted by the incongruity of having her sit in his office which was so distant from her comfort zone.

'No, it's not.'

'She's suitable.' Luiz delivered this with scathing honesty. Cecelia was eminently suitable and, the sooner that message was received by whatever rebellious bit of his brain insisted on telling him otherwise, the better.

'Your family must be very pleased. You told me that your father had been so keen to see you settle down.'

'Did I? I can't remember.' He had told her lots of things. They had talked a lot. She had always enjoyed talking. He once thought that she could coax anyone out of a bad mood with her cheerful chatter. 'Furthermore, I don't see where this is going. If you're not here for a hand out then what are you here for?'

'What I'm about to say to you might come as a bit of a shock, but I just want you to know that I'm very happy for you; happy that you've found someone...' It physically hurt to say that but say it she did, partly because she knew that she had to be dignified, given the situation, partly because she didn't want him to feel responsible for her when she told him what she had to.

Luiz stilled. For once he was at a complete loss. Was she ill? Panic flared inside him, obliterating every thought and every feeling.

'I'm pregnant, Luiz. I wish there was a kinder way of telling you, but I can't think of any.'

It took a few seconds for his wayward brain to catch up with what she had just said. In fact, even when it did catch up, Luiz didn't believe that he had heard correctly. His body was tense as he leaned forward, hands flat on the desk, and looked at her with frowning intensity.

'Sorry. Repeat that. I don't think I quite caught what you said...'

'I'm having a baby.'

'No. No, you're wrong. You can't be.' He was overwhelmed by a sensation of unreality. He wondered if he might be hallucinating.

'The doctor thinks it might have happened that weekend of the party. I was sick, do you remember? Apparently there's a chance of the contraceptive failing if you're sick. I never noticed anything, because as soon as we broke up I came off the pill and I just assumed that I hadn't had a period because my body was adjusting. Okay, so I was putting on a bit of weight, but I was eating more. I only found out a few days ago when I went to the doctor. The thing is, he did a check and there's no doubt.'

Her voice was calm and level but she had had a few days to think about it all, to come to terms with her life never being the same again. She had already gone past that state of shock which she could now see Luiz experiencing as his healthy golden colour turned ashen and he stared at her, not really focusing.

'I don't believe you.' But again his eyes were drawn to the fulsome curves which the shapeless sack dress was keen to conceal. She wouldn't lie. He heavily admitted to himself that she was nothing like Clarissa.

'Look, I know you're involved with someone else, and I haven't come here to try and…and ruin anything for you.'

'You tell me you're pregnant and then say that you don't want to *ruin anything for me?*'

Holly flushed but maintained eye contact. 'I didn't have to come,' she said quietly. 'In fact, for a while I was tempted not to, but I thought that you deserved to at least know the truth. I don't expect you to do anything about it and I don't want anything from you. I just felt that it was important for you to…to know.' She stood up and nervously wiped her clammy hands on her dress.

'Where the hell do you think you're going? You can't come in here and drop a bombshell and then leave!'

'It's a bombshell for you, Luiz, but not for me—and, before you even think about asking me to get rid of it, then *don't*.'

'I would *never* ask you to do such a thing.'

'And don't think about lumping me in the same bracket as your ex-girlfriend, either. I really *am* pregnant. I've had a scan. I can show it to you if you like. It dates the pregnancy. It's confirmed. Plus, like I said, I don't want anything from you. I don't want your money and I don't want you thinking that you have to be responsible for accidentally creating a life when you had no plans to. I'm going to go now and leave you to think this over. You might want to tell your fiancée, spare her the shock of finding out later down the line.'

The word 'fiancée' failed to register. Luiz was fired with an overwhelming urge to glue her to the chair and make her keep talking while he harnessed his thoughts and started thinking rationally. No part of his brain was functioning the way it normally did. Hell, *he was going to be a father!*

His eyes dipped to her stomach, back up to those swollen breasts that should have alerted him to the possibility that this was her news, the reason for her sudden appearance. What on earth had possessed him to think that she would suddenly discover the need to fleece him? She had never given a damn about material things. Was he so cynical that, the second she knew the truth about him, he could see no option other than pigeon-holing her? He might be wrong, of course, but now, with a baby inside her—*his baby*—he no longer had the luxury of disposing of her to protect himself from any possible threat of opportunism.

But she was already heading out of the door.

'Just think about what I've said, Luiz. I'll be in London until tomorrow and, if you want to talk some more, then that's fine. You have my mobile number. Unless, of course, you've deleted it…'

He looked like death warmed up. She thought that he must truly feel as though his world had imploded, as though his worst nightmare had come true. 'Right now, I don't want you to follow me and I don't want you to try and make me stay here. I've said what I've come to say and I'm leaving now.'

# CHAPTER FIVE

HOW COULD SHE sail into his office, make an announcement that was going to blow his world apart and then sail right out, having forbidden him from following her? Or at the very least from locking her in his office and compelling her to repeat herself until his brain began truly absorbing what she had said.

Even as she disappeared through his office door, Luiz knew that it would be a mistake to try and drag her back. Despite her sunny nature, she could be stubborn, and he recognised that closed expression on her face and the thin, determined line of her mouth. It was the same look she had worn when, months previously, an itinerant worker had come to the sanctuary to reclaim the dog he had been caught beating. She had told him to get lost and he had taken one look at that obstinate face and had done as he had been ordered. Luiz had been impressed. He was rather less impressed now, when the stubborn determination was directed at him.

He was going to be a father. He could pretend that she might be lying, but not even he, sceptic that he was, could kid himself on that score. It was a messy situation, but in the quiet of his office, with all calls on hold and all meetings cancelled—much to his secretary's surprise—Luiz recognised that it was not a situation that was going to go away despite what Holly had defiantly said. The mere fact that she had sought him out was indication enough that she now acknowledged that he was an indispensable part of her life. Talk about him having choices, about him being able to walk away, was empty talk. She surely must know that that would never be an option.

Whether she would ever admit it or not, she had landed on her feet in the money stakes.

He called her just before he was ready to leave the office. It was a little after five, hours before his normal departure time, but he hadn't been able to focus on anything. She had asked him to mull things over. As far as he was concerned he had devoted the necessary time to the task at hand.

'We need to meet.'

Holly heard the peremptory command in his voice and shivered. 'Okay.'

'Where are you staying?'

She gave him the name and address of the hotel. No one could accuse it of being five-star. It might struggle to make two, in fact.

Just out of the shower, she looked at the shabby wallpaper, the uninspiring prints on the wall and the snap-together furniture.

'That part of London is a dump. Couldn't you have found anywhere a little more upmarket?'

'This wasn't meant to be a weekend break,' Holly retorted. 'I had to come to London, so I chose somewhere affordable.'

'I will send my driver for you...'

'If you tell me where you want to meet,' Holly interjected, just in case he thought that she would be impressed by a driver, 'I can take public transport.'

Luiz ignored that. 'He will be with you in half an hour.'

'Luiz...'

'Don't be proud, Holly. I have a driver and it will save

you the hassle of taking the tube or a bus. We'll talk when
we meet.'

Autocratic and controlling, Holly thought as she discon-
nected. And yet, hadn't he always been? When they had
been going out together, he had always known what to do
in any crisis. He had always made decisions with an assur-
ance that made you believe that there could not be any other
possible outcome than the one he dictated. She had thrilled
at his intuitive mastery, which was what she now suddenly
decided to label arrogance.

Having put on weight, and having now found out that she
was pregnant, Holly had abandoned all attempts to squeeze
into her normal jeans and had invested in a couple of loose
dresses. The one she now put on was slightly less frumpy
than the one in which she had travelled and, despite her
blistering scorn for Luiz and the lies he had told her, she
still found herself surreptitiously eyeing her reflection in
the mirror.

She didn't think she looked pregnant. Not really. Perhaps
a bit in profile; she looked at herself sideways on and placed
her hand flat on her stomach. She looked…fat.

The shock of discovering herself to be pregnant had very
quickly been replaced with joy, despite the obvious pitfalls
ahead. Never had she wanted something as much as she
wanted this baby. It might be Luiz's nightmare, but not for
her.

With this in mind, she anxiously climbed into the back
seat of the top-of-the-range car which arrived to collect her
precisely when Luiz had told her it would. It was only once
she was inside the car that she realised she had forgotten to
ask him where, exactly, they would be meeting.

Anticipating a restaurant, she was taken aback when the
driver pulled away from the main drag to manoeuvre the
leafy streets of Chelsea. She was even more taken aback

when they finally stopped in front of an impressive four-storeyed red-brick building fronted by elaborately moulded wrought-iron gates. Two art deco stone lions, each slightly under a metre high, sat on either side of the black front door.

She had seen his office. Now she was going to see his house. She felt a nervous flutter and staunchly reminded herself that they were no longer lovers. They were now two people unhappily bound by circumstance.

The driver discreetly melted away the minute Luiz was in the hallway. For a few seconds, Holly could only stare. He was in a pair of faded black jeans that emphasised the length and muscular strength of his legs, and a dark-grey polo shirt. He was barefoot because the warm wooden floors were liberally broken with silk rugs which she imagined were sensuously soft to walk on.

It was an effort to tear her eyes away from him so that she could inspect her surroundings. Having braced herself for whatever further signs of this life he had been living away from her, she was still shocked at the visible extent of his wealth.

Bold paintings adorned the pale walls. Behind him, spanning a floor and a half, light filtered through an awe-inspiring stained-glass window. In various directions she could see further evidence of the wealthy background he had kept such a closely guarded secret from her. More paintings on the walls, a plant the size of a small tree strategically placed in the corner of a room, the merest glimpse of a sunken sitting area in what appeared to be a massive drawing room.

Holly was reluctantly forced to concede, just for a few seconds, that here was a man who might be über-cautious when it came to trust, especially in view of his past experience at the hands of a gold-digger.

'If you're going to give me a lecture on what a lowlife I

am for hiding all this from you, then let's get it out of the way so that we can move on to more important issues.'

'It's a very impressive house.'

'Take off the coat.'

'I beg your pardon?'

'I want to see evidence of your pregnancy.'

'You mean you actually don't believe that I'm telling you the truth?'

'I do.' He strolled towards her to ease her out of the coat and then, still standing in front of her, he gently rested his hand on her stomach.

The gesture came from nowhere and was so shocking that Holly gasped and stared up at him with huge, rounded eyes.

'Well?' Luiz moved back to thrust his hands into his pockets. Touching her like that, he could feel the firmness of her belly, the swell of it as his flesh and blood grew inside her. It was a sensation like no other. 'Don't tell me I don't have a right to do that.'

'We no longer have…that sort of relationship, Luiz.' One feathery touched that had barely lasted two seconds and she could feel her body revving into life, as if it had just been idling for the past few weeks, waiting for a foot to depress the accelerator so that it could get going, charge back to life! She stepped away from him but her heart was beating at a rate and she knew that she was bright red.

Luiz was finding it next to impossible to look at her without imagining her with her clothes off. He had felt her stomach. He would have liked to see it, smooth and full, just as he would have liked to see her breasts, more succulent, the nipples bigger and darker, readying themselves for a suckling baby.

'You said we…we needed to talk, Luiz, and we do—'

'I'll get you something to drink. Have you eaten?'

'I'm not hungry.'

'I'll order something in.'

'There's no need…'

'If we're going to have an argument every single time I suggest something, then we won't get very far,' Luiz said coolly. 'I lied to you—put it behind you and move on. Circumstances have now changed. There's no room for petty resentments.'

Holly bit back the torrent of self-defence that rose quickly to the surface. Arguing would be counter-productive. He was right and she knew that, but she still hated the cool detachment in his voice when he had addressed her. She was humiliatingly aware that *he* had moved on. For all the stern lectures she had given herself, she hadn't. It was easy for him to stand there and treat the whole matter like a business problem that required a solution—but then, little had she known it, he *was* a businessman who presumed that for every problem there was a solution. He was ideally placed to be dispassionate because he had no messy emotional ties to clutter the picture.

'Fine.' Holly managed the monosyllable but her voice sounded high and angry. He was heading towards the sitting room she had partially glimpsed through the half-opened door and she followed him, impervious to the grand displays of wealth.

The actual sitting area was an oasis of colour, sunken in the middle of an exquisite parquet surround, which was a suitable backdrop for beautifully maintained plants on one side and an imposing Chesterfield sofa on the other. Deep burgundy drapes pooled on the floor by the tall windows and picked up the rich colours of the sofas and the rug in the middle.

Luiz went immediately to one of the sofas and sprawled back. She had interrupted him in the middle of a drink. There was a bottle of red wine on the table in front of him, along with a crystal jug of iced water and a glass, presumably meant for her.

'Before you tell me that my life is going to remain exactly the same,' he drawled, his dark eyes fixed like lasers on her face, 'I should warn you that you'll be wasting your breath. Nothing in my life is going to be the same.'

'Nothing in *my* life is going to be the same, either!'

'And so we have to find a way of us both dealing with this situation.' Luiz leant forward to refill his glass. He had spent all afternoon thinking about this and the remorseless conclusion he had reached was that he would have to marry her. What choice did he have? He came from a traditional family. It might be perfectly acceptable for her to think that they could have some sort of informal arrangement whereby he popped in to visit his own child when and if he got the chance, maybe video-called if he couldn't be physically present. It wasn't going to work.

'I know it's going to be difficult,' Holly told him, 'But it's not that unusual a situation. You can come up whenever you want…have quality time. I won't interfere and I promise to be very accommodating. If, on the other hand, you'd rather not get involved to that extent, then that's fine as well. I understand that you've embarked on a whole new life with someone else and, although I do think it would be important for you to discuss this situation with your…er…girlfriend, there's no way I would expect anything from you.'

Luiz tilted his head to one side, for all the world as though he was paying keen attention and actually listening to what she was suggesting.

'No.'

'No? *No?* What do you mean *no?*' Holly looked at him in sudden confusion. She had exhausted all the options she could think of, so what exactly was he turning down? All of them? Didn't he know that there was nothing else on the table?

'I find that none of those options appeal.' He sighed, finding it fairly incredulous that she seemed to have bypassed the 'gold mine' option staring her in the face.

'I'm not following you.'

'Let me put it this way: as far as I am concerned, the only choice I have is to marry you. My child will be born legitimate; there's no other alternative. Naturally, you will have to agree to a pre-nup, but rest assured that as far as money goes you will be well taken care of. In fact, you could say that you will be rich beyond your wildest dreams.'

Holly was staring at him as though he had just grown wings and was now informing her that he would be flying to the moon. She wasn't sure that she had quite heard correctly. Marriage? Then, following on from that, a *pre-nup?*

Bright patches of angry colour stained her cheeks but she was determined to keep it together.

'That's impossible, Luiz.'

'You don't mean that.'

'But I do,' she ventured tightly. 'I could never forgive you for lying to me, Luiz, for assuming that I was an opportunist. Even when you got to know me, you still didn't feel that you could tell me the truth—and the fact that you can calmly sit there and talk about a pre-nup! Well, that just says it all, it really does.'

'Whether you like it or not,' Luiz's voice was low and firm, the voice of someone who has no intention of yielding, 'I am part of this equation, Holly. I didn't ask for this but I'm prepared to do the responsible thing.'

'I don't want you to feel responsible! I could never marry someone because they felt that it was their duty to marry me for the sake of a child!' Distraught, she jumped to her feet and paced the sitting area, glaring down at the ornate

Persian rug, unaware that Luiz was in front of her until she crashed into him and was forced to leap back.

She was hardly aware of his hands still steadying her. The deep, dark depths of his eyes held her captive and she knew that she was breathing quickly, practically hyperventilating. Like a moth helplessly drawn to a destructive flame, her mouth parted. She was aware of his touch altering, become more caressing. Of their own accord, her legs seemed to propel her inch by inch closer to him until they were separated by a hair's breadth.

'I don't just feel a sense of duty towards you,' Luiz murmured unsteadily.

Holly moaned. The soft sound shocked her, for it seemed to come from someone else, someone incapable of seeing reason.

Luiz's dormant libido was raging and all-consuming. That first feel of her lips against his was like manna from heaven and he lost himself in the kiss. At the same time he shakily pushed his hands underneath the dress. It was like touching her for the first time even though her body, satin-smooth beneath his exploring hands, was gloriously familiar.

Her breasts were heavy, spilling out of the bra which he deftly unclasped. He stifled a groan of pure pleasure as the abrasive pads of his thumbs found her nipples, and he began rubbing them ceaselessly, wanting nothing more than to get his mouth on them so that he could taste them.

'I want to see you.' His voice was rough and uneven.

'We shouldn't…' Holly could no longer think straight. The thought of seeing that flare of desire in his eyes as he looked at her threatened to turn her legs to jelly, but she wanted him so badly. She knew she shouldn't, but how could she begin to fight the waves of pleasure radiating through her body? She allowed herself to be gently propelled back towards the huge, deep-red velvet sofa and her knees buckled as she hit the edge of it. In a trance, she sank back and her breath caught in her throat as he unbuttoned the top half of her dress. With a whimper of reluctant, inevitable submission, her eyelids fluttered shut on the sight of him staring down at her exposed breasts, taking in the ripe curves of her newly pregnant body.

She had never been able to resist him and she still couldn't, Luiz thought with a savage surge of satisfaction. Despite all her protests, one touch and she melted. His arousal was pushing hard against the zip of his trousers but he took time to appreciate the stunning, glorious beauty of her incredible curves.

He didn't stop to question the mystery of his erratic libido. He just knew that he wanted her. She was carrying his baby! Suddenly, there was an eroticism to that notion that left him reeling. He had never thought about having children before and yet, with the evidence of his virility in front of him, he was unashamedly proud of his achievement.

He felt her wriggle and writhe under him as he ran his hand over her stomach and marvelled at the sensuous feel of its roundness. He was strangely blown away to think that the miracle of life was happening under his hand. He was utterly lost in the anticipation of taking her, having inhabited a sex-free zone ever since he had walked out of her house, when he heard the sound of his doorbell.

Holly had sank so fast and so deep into the whirlpool of exquisite sensation that it took her sluggish brain a few seconds to realise that someone was at the door. Reality pushed through and she struggled onto her elbows. She was horrified at how easily she had succumbed to Luiz's advances. What had she been thinking?

This was a man whose only concern lay with money; who had lied to her and then compounded his lack of faith in her by proposing marriage preceded by a pre-nup, which was the ultimate declaration that he still felt his wealth had to be protected! This was someone who would never have sought her out, would have been happy never to lay eyes on her again had she not turned up on his doorstep. A man who had grudgingly seen no other option for dealing with a situation he didn't want but to marry her out of a misplaced sense of responsibility. On all fronts, a man from whom she should be keeping a healthy distance unless strictly necessary. And, yet, she had flung herself in his arms at the slightest of provocations!

As far as Holly was concerned, Luiz thought that he could always get exactly what he wanted and he wanted to marry her because, really and truly, he wanted the child she was carrying. She had turned down his marriage proposal. Had he then decided that there was more than one way of getting what he wanted, and having her back in his bed might succeed where words had failed? Once she had been his for the asking. Did he think that nothing had changed?

How genuine could his so-called sudden attraction be when he hadn't made the slightest effort to get in touch for all those weeks, when in fact he had already found himself…

Shame and dismay left her speechless as she suddenly remembered that he had a girlfriend, the beautiful, glamorous Cecelia. So swept away had she been, that only now as the doorbell rang once more with renewed insistence, did she recall the leggy brunette with the impeccable connections.

Watching her, Luiz could easily see what was going through Holly's head and he cursed fluidly under his breath.

'Ignore that,' he commanded, running with the theory that if he gave her no chance to withdraw completely from him then he could woo her back to the place which he was now desperate for her to occupy.

'I can't believe you. You…' She wriggled, yanking up her dress and manoeuvring herself out from underneath him.

'Let's not play the blame game here, Holly. You haven't ended up naked and under me because there was a gun to your head.'

'And do you think I respect myself for…for…?'

'Just come right out and say it—for wanting to make love to me. Where's the shame in that?' The doorbell rang again and Luiz furiously levered himself up while Holly frantically tried to get herself in order.

She was running her fingers through her hair when she heard the clicking of heels on the wooden floor, and when she looked to the doorway it was to see the most beautiful woman she had ever seen in her life. A living, breathing fashion doll was staring down at her.

Cecelia Follone. In real life, she was a million times more drop-dead gorgeous than the grainy pictures on the Internet had suggested. Long, dark hair flowed in artful disarray down her slender back. Olive-skinned and green-eyed, she had a body that was made for very, very small items of clothing, and she clearly knew that, for the vibrant red jersey-dress barely skimmed the top of her thighs. She carried her expensive coat over one shoulder.

For a few seconds, both were speechless for different reasons, but Cecelia was the first to break the silence with a barrage of high-pitched, accusatory Portuguese. Holly didn't have to be a mind-reader to understand exactly what was being said. Mortified, she hurried up to the doorway, her face burning and her eyes very pointedly not resting on Luiz who seemed remarkably unfazed by the arrival of his girlfriend. He held up one imperious hand which brought the torrent of rapid Portuguese to an abrupt halt.

'It seems I have forgotten that I had a date…understandable, given the circumstances.'

Holly took a deep breath and held out her hand to Cecelia who looked at it disparagingly. 'I…I'm very pleased to meet you.' She dropped her hand to her side and cleared her throat. 'I'm…eh…Holly.'

This elicited another round of hysterical Portuguese which Luiz listened to before saying coldly, 'Please speak English, Cecelia.'

'Who are you and what are you doing here?'

'Actually, I was just on my way out.'

'I don't think so…' Luiz's voice was calm and final but Holly ignored him.

'I came here to…to…'

'Circumstances have changed, Cecelia.' Luiz turned to the brunette who in heels was easily six feet, which made Holly feel like a pygmy in comparison. 'I will call you tomorrow to explain but I'm afraid I'm going to have to ask you to leave now.'

'I am not going anywhere until I know what is going on!' Cecelia's high-pitched, accented English was laced with venom.

'Nothing's going on!' Holly defended quickly. 'I just came to have a quick chat with, er, Luiz, and I was just about to leave.'

'Chat about what?'

Luiz had been lounging against the doorway, and with a laborious sigh he swivelled Cecelia to face him and spoke to her in Portuguese. He kept his voice low and flat which made much more of an impact than if he had shown any sign of emotion.

From the sidelines, Holly watched as Cecelia's eyes widened and her mouth compressed. She wanted to be anywhere but here, in this house, and she was sickeningly ashamed of herself and of her lack of self-control. Trying to make herself as invisible as she could, staring down at the floor, she kept perfectly still for the next ten minutes as Luiz and Cecelia conducted a conversation she couldn't understand but was astute enough to surmise.

She breathed a sigh of relief when Cecelia was finally escorted out of the house and she took advantage of that brief window of time alone to gather all her possessions so that she was ready and waiting to leave when Luiz re-entered the room.

'What did you say to her?' Holly asked bluntly.

'Where are you going? Our conversation isn't finished by a long way. I told Cecelia that our relationship was over.'

'Because of me?'

'I didn't go into details but, considering you were standing in a state of dishevelment right in front of her, then I'm guessing she might have deduced the reasons for herself.'

'How could you? How could you seduce me when you're involved with someone else? It makes me feel ill to think about it.' She felt even more ill as she wondered when he had last made love to Cecelia. Yesterday? The day before? Every day for the last few weeks they had been dating? He was a very virile man with a powerful libido. She couldn't bear the thought of him touching the other woman and then touching her, and she was shocked at the force of her own jealousy which had no part to play in the sort of relationship they now had.

Luiz hesitated. Getting rid of Cecelia, callous though he knew he must appear, had not been any great hardship. She had occupied the strange void left in Holly's absence and he was disturbed at himself for allowing that to happen. He wondered how he couldn't have seen that, however great her credentials, she still didn't quite fit the bill. He pulled back from the question he knew Holly was asking him—had Cecelia been his lover?—as his sex life wasn't under discussion here. It was an irrelevance. The fact that he hadn't had one with Cecelia was an even greater irrelevance as far as he was concerned.

'My relationship with Cecelia is no longer an issue. Reaching a conclusion on how to deal with what has happened *is*. So...' He nodded in the direction of the lounge. Holly hesitated, adamant that she had put her cards on the table and was not going to reshuffle the deck and start again. More than anything, she needed to make him understand that that little blip when she had fallen straight back into his arms was not going to happen again. She reluctantly removed the coat and followed him into the sitting room.

'You didn't have to break up with your girlfriend,' were her opening words as she sat down, facing him. 'I told you I didn't want to ruin anything you had with her and I meant it.'

'In that case, you are clearly a lot more liberated than I am.' He folded his arms behind his head. 'Somehow going out with one woman whilst another is having my baby doesn't work for me.' He dropped his arms to his knees and leaned forward. 'Don't try and fight me on this, Holly. Marriage is the only solution. I will not be a part-time father and it would be immoral to deprive any child of the benefit of having two parents.'

'And it wouldn't be right for us to get married just for the sake of a child. Luiz, you never, ever wanted any sort of commitment with me. You never trusted me. How on earth can you expect me to ignore all of that and to get married just because of an accident?'

'Tripping over a loose paving stone is an accident; the ramifications disappear quickly. Having a child is in a completely different league and the ramifications never disappear. Whatever the circumstances of this pregnancy, we both have to take ownership of the situation and bury our differences.'

Talking to him, Holly thought helplessly, was like talking to a brick wall. Yet there was no way that she was going to cave in. As far as she was concerned, they could both be loving parents without having to pay the ultimate price. She wanted to tell him that, had it not been for the life growing inside her, he would have already been making plans to marry Cecelia. He would have had his perfect partner. Now, he would be stuck with her, and how long before the poisonous thread of resentment began seeping into him?

'That doesn't mean that we have to get married.' Holly looked at him with stubborn defiance. 'We can be loving, responsible parents without being tied to one another. It's better that we're both happy individuals apart than miserable and bitter together.'

Luiz didn't see how she could possibly mean that when less than three months ago she had been keen to take their relationship to another level. Yet, that stubborn, closed expression...

For the first time he fully appreciated the depth of the damage his well-intentioned fabrications had done. Throw in a girlfriend acquired for all the wrong reasons and, no matter that the girlfriend had been dispatched and marriage proposed, she was still in no mood to budge.

'You make it sound as though marriage to me would be torture,' Luiz said through gritted teeth, frustrated at being unable to get around her. 'And yet, don't try and pretend that there isn't chemistry between us!'

'I wondered how long it would take for you to bring that up!' Holly retorted with bitterness. Sex was all it had ever been for him. While she had been busy building castles in the sky and fantasising about marriage and babies, he had been happy to use her as a plaything, a doting plaything willing to do anything he wanted.

'Yes, I find you attractive. I suppose lots of women do. It's not enough.' She lowered her eyes. There was a treacherous voice in her head asking her what was enough, really? Were there ever any guarantees that any marriage would work out…? Didn't some marriages fail even when the right boxes had all been ticked and the profit-and-loss columns neatly balanced…?

She ignored that voice and continued quietly and insistently, 'We both deserve happiness. You shouldn't have broken up with your girlfriend. One day, I'll find my soul mate and it will be healthier for our child to be the products of two happy parents even if they're not happy together.'

Luiz was affronted by what she had just said on pretty much every level. Whatever he had said or done in the past, most other women would have leapt at the offer he had extended because it really didn't get much better than that. The fact that they still couldn't keep their hands off one another was an added and pleasurable bonus. So why was she digging her heels in and treating him as though he had offered her a pact with the devil? And who was this *soul mate* she had in mind? Not too long ago, *he* had been her soul mate! Why couldn't she stop being so damned proud and wake up to the fact that he was right?

'Ending my relationship with Cecelia was not a source of regret for me,' Luiz conceded heavily. 'I would have broken up with her whether or not you were in the picture.'

'You would?' Holly could have kicked herself for the spark of interested curiosity she could hear in her voice. Did that make any difference? No. 'But she's perfect for you. I thought you were on the lookout for the right woman with the right background…'

'We're covering old ground here. You won't marry me—that poses a number of obvious problems. Firstly, do you honestly expect me to commute to Yorkshire?'

'You did for ages.' She was afflicted with a sharp pang

of memory at the pleasure those weekend visits had always elicited.

'Weekends.' Luiz brushed aside her interruption dismissively. 'I would want more than just weekend visits. It is a long way to travel for a couple of hours during the week. Furthermore, what about schooling when the time comes? How far is it to the nearest school? Do you suggest an erratic education because you live in the middle of nowhere where it's liable to snow for a large proportion of winter?'

'You're projecting into the future,' Holly said uncertainly.

'I'm attempting to reach a fair and equitable arrangement. Sacrifices have to be made. If you're not willing to marry me, then you're going to have to climb down from your moral platform and start meeting me halfway.'

'I can't live in a city.'

'And I refuse to commute to Yorkshire. It's impractical.' If she wanted to play hardball, Luiz thought, then he would play hardball, too.

'Why do you have to be unreasonable?' But was he? How many men would have risen to the occasion with equal unstinting generosity? He hadn't asked for his life to be derailed by circumstances beyond his control and yet he was willing to assume his responsibilities whatever the cost to the future he had had neatly laid out in front of him. In return, all she could think about was her own past hurt and emotional wounds that were still raw and bleeding. She sighed and slumped. 'I can't move to a city—what about my animals?' she asked in a small voice.

'This can all be worked out.' He refused to yield to her drooping, forlorn body language. 'I'll be out of the country for the next week. You can use the time to think about it. You seem to think that nothing will change—everything will.'

# CHAPTER SIX

AFTER THE DRAMA of London, returning to the tranquillity of the countryside failed to deliver the peace Holly had banked on. She had too much on her mind. Her thoughts were all over the place. She wanted to be honest with herself, yet found it impossible to leave her bitter grievances behind. She told herself that she hated Luiz and yet she knew that she was still as fiercely attracted to him as she had been in the thick of their relationship. There was no way that she could ever turn the clock back and love him... Yet a demanding voice inside her insisted that, if she didn't still have feelings for him, then why was it that she couldn't accept his marriage proposal which was fair and made sense? Surely if she wasn't emotionally invested then, like him, she would be able to deal with the situation in a detached, pragmatic and sensible manner?

She could reluctantly see that her location would not be convenient for him. She didn't want to leave her friends and her sanctuary behind, yet the need for compromise weighed heavily on her shoulders.

'You should just marry him,' Andy told her bluntly when she offloaded all her thoughts on him the evening after she had returned to her cottage. They were at her kitchen table and outside the greyest of days had slipped into starry night. Through the kitchen window, with the curtains open, a full moon illuminated the fields and open countryside. In the depths of winter, these same fields could be snow-covered for days on end… How on earth would Luiz be able to get up to see his child? For an hour or two? Sometimes, the sanctuary could be cut off for a week…longer…then what? Would she find herself in the constant line of fire for failing to compromise?

'Let's think pros and cons. He's dishy, he's the catch of the century… Frankly, my dear, if you won't have him, then I will.' Andy sniggered at his own joke. 'But, seriously, having a kid…it's not ideal in a place as remote as this, sweetie. Think illness and having to get hold of a doctor. Think having friends over after playschool; what do you do with them when it's time for them to go and it's started snowing—stash them in with Buster the donkey?'

'You're supposed to be on my side,' Holly grumbled.

'I don't think anyone wins medals for being stubborn.'

'I'm not being stubborn.' For 'stubborn' Holly read 'selfish'. 'I have a right to a life here, where I know everyone. I have my livelihood here. What would happen to this animal sanctuary if I left?'

'I don't think the animals would all pack their bags and leave home,' Andy told her with brutal honesty. 'It's a very viable proposition. You would be able to sell it, along with the cottage and the land, and you'd get a good price for it. And there's something I've been meaning to tell you…'

Holly looked at him warily. He had changed out of his grubby work clothes into a clingy checked top and black jeans. She didn't like the way he was scrupulously inspecting the tips of his cowboy boots, avoiding her eyes.

'Remember Marcus?'

'How could I forget your broken heart?' Holly asked wryly.

'He's back from Toronto,' Andy said sheepishly. 'We've

been emailing. I didn't want to make anything of it in case it didn't work out but he's packed in the job over there and has taken up a residency at Guy's Hospital in London.'

'And…?' But Holly already knew what he was going to say. Andy and Marcus had been an item before Marcus had relocated to Toronto, on his own, because Andy had refused to go with him. Now he was being given a second shot at the relationship and he was going to move to London.

She would be on her own. She listened, smiling and nodding encouragingly as Andy told her all about his plans. They had seen a house. It would be perfect and he was thinking of teaching as a career. Her mind was suddenly in a daze. Without Andy, the sanctuary just wouldn't be quite the same, yet she refused to see capitulation to Luiz as the only option.

If she removed that awful, swoony feeling she got whenever she was in his presence, then what was she left with? A man who was prepared to 'do the right thing'. She couldn't help but wonder, if she married him, how long he would carry on being prepared to do the right thing. He didn't love her, so how on earth could he ever hope to remain faithful to her? Would part of any union between them be the tacit understanding that he could continue seeing other women, women like Cecelia, just as long as he didn't flaunt his infidelities? Did he imagine that a sham marriage was better than no marriage at all?

Andy's imminent departure seemed to raise more questions about her own situation than she felt she could reasonably deal with and she spent a restless night, only managing to fall properly asleep in the early hours of the morning and awakening, muddle-headed, to the sound of the dogs going wild in their compound.

In fact, hurriedly getting dressed and heading down the stairs, it dawned on her that the commotion went beyond the barking of dogs. Flinging open the front door, she was confused to see three cars parked at haphazard angles in front of the enclosures. Andy was not yet on the scene, but Claire and Sarah, two of the girls who helped out, were and they seemed to be in awkward conversation with a handful of men. Altogether, it was a bewildering scene, and as Holly remained in the doorway, trying to assimilate what was going on, she was spotted.

Like a rabbit caught in the headlights of a speeding car, she froze to the spot. Her sluggish brain computed that two more cars were speeding up the winding drive, doors opening even before the cars had pulled to a stop. She had no idea what was going on. Claire and Sarah were running full tilt towards her.

'You dark horse!' Claire was laughing. 'You never told us that you were getting married to a billionaire!'

It dawned on Holly what was going on pretty much when the questions started being shouted at her, intrusive questions bombarding her like bullets fired from a gun. She yanked Claire and Sarah into the house, slammed the front door and got on the phone to Andy. She told him he wasn't to come in; there were reporters everywhere.

He was thrilled, Holly a lot less so. Even Claire and Sarah, once she had briefed them on the situation, fell into a subdued silence. The cottage felt as though it was under siege. Holly drew the curtains in the sitting room so that the three of them were huddled like fugitives in the semi-darkness. Had they got the message and left? Or were they lurking outside like Rottweilers, ready to pounce? She didn't know.

She had never experienced anything like this in her life before. Doing a full day's work was out of the question. Never before had she questioned the origins of all those intrusive pictures she had seen in tacky magazines, where celebrities were caught in their least favourable moments.

Now, experiencing the horror of the paparazzi in full pursuit, she felt a grudging sympathy for them.

Frustrated and angry, she left Claire and Sarah gossiping in the sitting room and headed for the kitchen, where once again she had to drop the roller blind before she could be guaranteed privacy for the phone call she had to make.

Luiz picked up on the third ring and Holly wasted no time telling him what was going on.

'I can't even go outside!' she screeched down the line. 'This is all your fault and you have to make them go *away!*'

On the other side of the Atlantic, Luiz was fully alert to the panic in her voice, despite the fact that the beep of his mobile had dragged him out of sleep. He was not in the slightest bit irritated by the phone call. Actually, he had been expecting it.

'Paparazzi are the bane of my life,' he told her, strolling across to the window from which he had an incomparable view of New York's Central Park. Even at this hour, it seemed to be humming with life. This was a city where no one ever seemed to sleep and, whilst he had always found that an appealing trait, mirroring his own continual restlessness, he had been missing London and anticipating the next step in sorting out the situation that had landed on his doorstep with Holly.

'I don't *care* about that!' Holly wailed. 'I can't get outside and I don't know what to do! This is really the last straw, Luiz—why are they here? How did they even find out about us? They've been asking all sorts of questions about the pregnancy! Have you said something to them? They're like bloodhounds! No, I take that back—that would be an insult to bloodhounds!'

'Are you sitting down?'

'You don't sound in the least bit bothered!' Holly ignored his question. Whilst she had been screaming like an enraged banshee, his tone of voice had been mild and unruffled. As it would be, she thought sourly, because *he* wasn't the one having to endure a clutch of strangers with microphones hiding out in the shrubbery! Sooner or later, Claire and Sarah would have to go. They would be pursued, would probably love their fifteen minutes of fame and within seconds her story would have spread like wildfire through all the neighbouring villages and towns. That was how it worked in this part of the world. Lots of people knew her, had known her parents. She detested the thought of having her privacy invaded, her situation discussed and analysed on receipt of third-hand information. She was fully prepared to let Luiz take the blame for that occurrence.

'I've had my fair share of nosy reporters. I've learnt how to deal with them.'

'How?' Holly practically shrieked.

'Ignore them. If they ask any questions, just say "no comment". They can only carry on hounding you for so long if you don't give them any information to play with. Sooner or later they'll get bored and give up.'

'It sounds easier said than done,' Holly imparted gloomily but she was no longer shaking like a leaf in a high wind. 'And you never told me how they found me...'

'I think we can call that Cecelia's parting gift for me.' Luiz had suspected that the paparazzi might descend. He had received a phone call from his ex only hours before he had left London, to be told that she had spoken to friends, including a certain journalist who was always eager for celebrity news and always keen to unearth details about him. It had taken Luiz all of two seconds to suspect that their break-up would have had him drooling with curiosity, particularly when he heard all the details, for she had guessed an unforeseen pregnancy and had hit jackpot, although her pathway to that conclusion had been highly illogical.

'You would never go out with someone as fat as that,' she had said maliciously. 'Which means that the stupid cow must be pregnant. I hope you're pleased with yourself, Luiz! You could have had me and instead you've landed a nobody who'll probably fleece you! And just wait until your family hears!'

They hadn't heard yet but it wouldn't be long. Making that call and announcing the news that would inevitably reach them was not something Luiz was looking forward to. He suspected that he would have to weather his sisters' jibes and the annoying comparisons they would make with Clarissa. His mother might be more lenient on that score, or at least would keep her opinions to herself, but the lack of plans for a wedding would upset her.

'I don't know what to do,' Holly admitted, at the end of her tether. 'I can't go outside and see about the animals without being accosted. Claire and Sarah are in my sitting room but they can't stay here all day. I've told Andy not to bother coming in.'

'I guess he would have been upset at that,' Luiz said absently, revealing how much he knew Andy and his endearingly preening ways whenever there was the slightest chance of a camera being pointed in his direction. 'You can send Claire and Sarah out to see to the animals. Just make sure they don't open their mouths. They're responsible enough to keep quiet and they'll probably enjoy the attention. You can send them out in a couple of hours' time.'

'Why then?'

'Because I can't work instant miracles from the other side of the world!

'I'm not asking you to work miracles!'

'Yet you telephone me in a rage to complain about your privacy being invaded even though you must surely know that I'm not in the country. Either you just wanted to make sure you realised how much you blame me for reporters in your back garden or else, deep down, you trust me to sort it out for you.'

Did she trust him to sort it out? What did that say about her, when she should have been planning a life of independence? When she had rejected his offer to kindly shackle himself to her for the sake of a pregnancy he hadn't asked for?

'It's not a matter of trust,' Holly prevaricated tersely. 'I didn't know who you were when we were going out. Having a bunch of reporters on my land taking pictures and badgering me for answers about what's going on between us isn't my fault. You're the one with the big reputation and the gossip-column lifestyle. I phoned you because this would never have happened if it hadn't been for you.'

'What are you saying?'

'I'm saying that I don't like these people hanging around my house. I like my privacy. I'm saying that I wished I'd never met you.' Never had a few simple words cut through her like those did. The silence strummed between them, the tension heightened by the fact that she couldn't see his face, couldn't read the expression on it.

But she didn't take the words back. More than anything, she desperately wanted to make him see that she wasn't a doll he could control—that the Holly of old who had absolutely adored him was not the Holly of the here and now who carried the hurt of knowing that he wouldn't have come near her with a bargepole if she had known the extent of his wealth and influence. Who knew that, whatever arrangement he wanted, more than anything else he wanted to make sure that she couldn't have a hold over his money.

Luiz was cold with anger at this surly display of petulance. With the hard, inescapable force of logic, however, he was compelled to concede that if they had never met she would probably be married to a local guy by now, someone unchallenging who went to the pub with his mates every Friday, held a season ticket to see the local football club and saved for a two-week holiday somewhere in sunny Spain.

It irked the hell out of him to think that she might actually have been happier with someone like that. He might have given her memorable and unforgettable nights; he might have made her body sing; they might have travelled down a thousand conversational highways and byways—but, in the end, he had lied to her and in the face of that everything they had shared was reduced to rubble. Free from the pressure of being a billionaire with a reputation, he had given her more than he could remember giving any other woman, yet she could still tell him in that flat, detached voice that she wished she had never met him.

He wanted to remind her that, lies or no lies, there was no other woman he could think of who wouldn't have jumped at the chance of being his wife. He wanted to tell her that a pre-nup, against which she seemed to be unreasonably biased, was an insignificant technicality which would certainly not affect the financial comforts she would enjoy as his wife. But he suspected that she would find a way of throwing that back in his face.

'You might want to remember that there are two of us stuck here,' Luiz drawled. 'My life has been equally devastated but hurling accusations at one another isn't going to solve anything.'

In a heartbeat, Holly recognised what he was really saying. That, however much she claimed to regret ever having met him, the feeling was mutual. If he hadn't met her, slept with her and had a pointless affair with her, he would not have landed up in a nightmarish parallel universe where life as he knew it was over. Having engineered the opening attack, she was deeply hurt by his admission. Clutching the telephone in her hand, she just wanted the ground to open up and swallow her whole. Her mouth felt as though it was stuffed with cotton wool and her eyes were burning.

'Yes,' she said stiffly.

'So pack a couple of bags and arrange with Andy to come in later to see to the animals. I'll get my people to come and rescue you. They'll come via that dirt road across the fields that leads to the back of the cottage by the disused stable. You'll get a call from my man; his name is Nicholas. He'll call you when he's about to arrive and you can send Claire and Sarah out. They will distract the reporters and you can slip out through the back door.'

'I hate this cloak-and-dagger stuff...'

'In which case, you can brave the paparazzi and their cameras and find yourself in tomorrow's sleazy tabloid.'

'How come none of this ever happened before?'

'Because a high-profile billionaire businessman, a ditched ex-girlfriend who mixes with celebrities and a pregnant mistress looking after animals in the middle of nowhere has much more sale appeal than a guy who goes away for weekends. Reporters don't follow trails unless they think the trail is going to lead them somewhere. In the past, coming out to see you at the weekends, I was under the radar. I wasn't doing anything they cared about.'

'And what happens next—after I've abandoned my life to get out of the spotlight? When am I going to be able to return?'

Luiz's mouth thinned. 'Abandoned' was an emotive word. It would have been hard for her to make it any clearer that she didn't want him in her life. Tough. Whether she liked it or not, he was in it and he wasn't going anywhere any time soon.

'Not in the foreseeable future,' he said, without bothering to beat around the bush.

'What does *that* mean?' Holly cried.

'This has all the makings of a soap opera and there's nothing the gossip pages love more than a soap. Knowing Cecelia, she will be only too happy to stoke the fire out of revenge if she thinks it'll make life difficult for me.'

Since when was it a crime to play a situation for his own gain? Luiz wondered. And this sudden development had the potential to work nicely for him. 'Vengeful ex and pregnant country mistress; well, what can I say? The story could run… and run…and run… You might just have to get used to your sanctuary being trashed by reporters…'

'But they'll get bored once I leave.'

'They'll wise up to where you are and hot tail it down to London. The second you try to make it back up north, they'll be in vigorous pursuit. You have no idea how determined a reporter can be once he thinks he's onto a story that could sell…'

Holly was getting more worried by the second. It was true. Some people never seemed to be out of the glossies. Was that because hard-nosed reporters wouldn't leave them alone? Was her life never going to return to normal?

'I suggest you get down here. You can stay at my place. I'll make sure that I leave America immediately and we can take things from there.'

'But what about my sanctuary?'

'Andy and the rest of your team can hold the fort. They're perfectly capable. Oh, and before I forget, pack thoroughly. Include a passport. You *have* got one, haven't you?'

'Of course I have!'

'Good, then bring it.'

'But why on earth…?' The question was left unanswered because Luiz was already informing her that he had to go, cutting short her curiosity and leaving her in a state of confusion and unrest.

Outside, judging from the quick peek through the curtains, the reporters seemed to be braced for the long haul and had retreated to their cars where they were lurking, smoking and chatting, having thoroughly disturbed her animals. The dogs were still barking, although less hysterically; the ducks were squawking and the various assortment of waifs and strays, from her donkey to the two pigs, were joining in the chorus.

Claire and Sarah were agog with excitement. Their eyes were like saucers. They both promised not to breathe a word to any of the reporters, and Holly trusted them both implicitly, but she could see that if this was their reaction then Luiz had hit the nail on the head when he had told her that their story could be fodder for nosy reporters.

As things stood, she had no option but to do as Luiz had suggested. Her immediate future was in his hands and, as she hurriedly packed a couple of bags, she feverishly wondered how things had come to this. She wondered what would have happened if she had never started pushing for more than was on offer. Would he have continued enjoying her enthusiastic, trusting, blind devotion until he got bored or decided that it was time to move on and find a proper candidate for a proper relationship, instead of a pathetic sap who was only cut out to be a fake girlfriend? How could you think you knew someone only to find out that the person you thought you had known was a chimera?

And now here she was, forced to do as he said because she couldn't face the prospect of having her life invaded. It was a horrible nightmare. Three hours later, when finally the wheels of motion were beginning to roll and Nicholas, Luiz's henchman, was ready for her, she had a splitting tension headache.

Sarah and Claire were thrilled to death at the prospect of running the gauntlet with the reporters, who they claimed were young and cute, and acting as decoys. It smacked of something out of a movie. They were ridiculously excitable, but the ploy worked, and for the next hour and a half Holly shared the same weird feeling that she was in a movie. The drive to the field, the helicopter ride, the silent drivers and, finally, the stealthy entrance into Luiz's house, all felt unreal. Her life was no longer her own. But once she was in the house she felt completely protected. Luiz had left a message on her phone, informing her that he would be in early the following morning.

*We'll take it from there,'* his message had read. Until he arrived, Holly explored the mansion he called home. It was a distraction from dealing with the tangle of thoughts whirring round and round in her head. The last time she had been in the house, she had barely noticed the surroundings. Now, as she took her time exploring the multitude of rooms, she could truly appreciate the grandeur. Even the smallest details screamed 'money'. There were no personal giveaways, no family pictures on display. The entire house could have been transposed into an upmarket lifestyle magazine and no one would have been able to guess the identity of its owner.

There was ample food in the fridge and, after a light meal, she retired upstairs to one of the guest bedrooms where she promptly fell into a deep, untroubled sleep. She was utterly exhausted. When she groggily surfaced hours later, it was to weak sunshine streaming through a crack in the curtains and, wriggling onto her side, to the sight of Luiz hunkered on a chair he had dragged and positioned next to the bed.

Disoriented, she could only stare for a few seconds. Had he just stepped into the house? He was in a pair of dark trousers and a white shirt, the sleeves of which he had shoved up to his elbows. She had to forcibly squash the rebellious bit of her mind that wanted to play with images of how those long fingers had touched her all over her body. Nostalgia for what now seemed like a time of innocence ripped through her and she had the strangest desire to burst into tears.

'How long have you been sitting there?' she asked instead, wriggling into a sitting position.

Thanks to the heavy curtains, it was still dark in the bedroom even though it was after ten, but not so dark that Luiz couldn't see how her body had changed. Sexual awareness leapt through him and he adjusted his position on the chair.

'Five minutes at the most.' He stood up, flexed his muscles and strolled across to the window. 'I came to wake you up but you were out for the count.'

'I was tired.'

'Understandable.' Luiz had had time to do some serious thinking on the trip back to London. The harder he looked at the situation, the more he was convinced that marrying Holly was inevitable and for the best. Her pathetic cry of wanting a soul mate had opened his eyes to the ugly fact that, when and if this soul mate showed up, he, Luiz, would be reduced to playing second fiddle to a stranger who would be on hand to make decisions on the future of his child.

An even darker thought had occurred to him. This pregnancy would make Holly an extremely wealthy single parent because, whether she liked it or not, any child of his would enjoy the benefits of his enormous wealth and, by extension, so would she. What was to stop some sleazy charmer with an eye to the main chance from cosying up to her? She was soft, not one of those women who would be able to spot a slimeball from a mile away. 'You're pregnant and you've been hounded out of your house by reporters. Those two things would be enough to exhaust anyone.'

'Are they… Have they followed me…?'

'I had my picture taken a few times in front of the house,' Luiz said with a shrug. 'But I have a few beefy security guards at my disposal. No one gets too near. Besides, they probably know that answering questions isn't my thing, which is why you make a much better target.'

'I haven't said a word to anyone!'

'And they won't give up until you do. These people can be determined when they're in pursuit of a story. It's their bread and butter. In fact, I could tell you some stories of friends who have had their lives wrecked by cameras poking through windows and telescopic lenses capturing each and every private moment…'

Holly blanched.

'I know.' Luiz oozed sympathy. 'It's a shocking thought but there's no point evading reality. I've phoned and explained the situation to Andy. He's going to take over running the place for the time being. You never told me that he had plans to move back down to London.'

'He and Marcus are getting back together.' Holly wondered what 'for the time being' meant.

'Yes. He explained. He's over the moon. I've offered him the temporary use of one of my apartments until he finds his feet.'

'And he's accepted?' Somehow that reeked of treachery. She knew that Andy had been bowled over when the truth about Luiz's background had surfaced, but to accept his handouts? Really?

'Why wouldn't he?' Luiz said carelessly. 'Not everyone's hung up on making judgement calls about someone's good character because they happen to be rich.'

Holly's lips thinned. She refrained from telling him that it was all right for Andy. *He* hadn't been lied to and deceived and told that he wasn't good enough for a relationship. Besides, Luiz Casella was a fine one to talk. Hadn't *he* made judgements about *her* based on her *lack* of money? Somehow she knew that to go down that road, however, would make her sound churlish and petty. Besides, how much mileage was there in opening up raw wounds over and over again?

'But that's besides the point. Did you bring your passport?'

'Yes, but you didn't explain why it was necessary.'

'You once said that we should go on holiday together.'

'That was when I thought we had a future. That was when I thought we could save up and take a trip abroad. Before I knew that saving up was something you didn't have to do. In fact, before I found out that all you had to do was snap your fingers and you could go wherever in the world you wanted.'

She flushed because the last thing she wanted was to sound like an embittered woman, frustrated and disillusioned because the guy she loved hadn't picked her for the last dance. 'Sorry,' she mumbled. 'I do realise that bickering isn't going to get us anywhere.'

'You need your passport because we're going abroad.'

It was something she had dreamed of. A trip away, just the two of them... It would have taken a lot of planning because she would have had to arrange supervision for her animals and—she had supposed at the time—he would have had to book time off with his boss. But the idea had never got off the ground.

Now she wondered, with his vast knowledge of the goings-on of the paparazzi, whether he had sidelined holiday chat because he hadn't wanted to risk her finding out who he really was. Reporters wouldn't have been interested in the Luiz Gomez he had claimed to be. At any rate, how ironic that her much wanted holiday with him had been suggested in these circumstances. How ironic that his suggestion of a holiday now had all the hallmarks of someone trying to run her life for her.

'I don't want to go abroad,' she said firmly.

'Your choice. If you want to take on the piranhas of the

journalistic world, then be my guest. I am tough enough to deal with whatever gets thrown at me in the press, but I don't think you are.'

'I'm not quite the fragile person I once was,' Holly informed him coolly and his mouth curved into a smile of pure amusement that instantly sent her zooming back to those halcyon days before the truth had come as a wedge between them.

'Energetic…carefree…sexy… Those are things that come to mind when I think about you,' Luiz murmured, still amused. 'Fragile, not so much. Tree trunks never stood a chance when it came to being cut down to size to feed your fire. It was just one of the things I liked about you. So, fragile? Maybe not…'

The way those dark eyes were lingering on her made every bit of her burn. Even as she was telling herself that to be told that she wasn't fragile was an insult, all she could think was that he had found her sexy. Not that she hadn't known. He might have kept his real identity locked away, but when it came to the physical side of their relationship there had been no doubt as to the genuine fervour of his responses. Even as she was sternly recognising that she had to detach herself from him, erect defences to protect herself, she was succumbing to the glorious melting feeling he had always been able to induce in her.

'That's not what I meant,' Holly said in a strangled voice while he continued to stare at her with that sexy half-smile, his head half-inclined. They were separated by the width of the room but her body was reacting as though he was right next to her, touching her. 'Where would we go?' She felt as jumpy as a cat on a hot tin roof when she thought about being alone with him, even though they had spent loads of time alone together.

'Some place where we can't be reached or spied on. Give

it a couple of weeks and our riveting saga will have been superceded by something more exciting. Reporters are a fickle bunch.'

'I feel as though I'm being steamrollered into this…' He had been the one she turned to for advice for so long that she automatically voiced her concern aloud. Luiz felt a heady sense of powerful satisfaction at that instinctive inclination to yield to him.

'Trust me,' he drawled lazily, pushing himself away from the window and strolling towards the door. 'It'll be for the best.'

# CHAPTER SEVEN

THERE WAS SO much Holly was finding out about this man she had spent nearly two years loving, yet it seemed that there was room to find out still more. Beyond the reality of his background and wealth, she was also discovering the reach of his power and how fast things could move if he so dictated. It seemed he had an army of people at the ready to turn his commands into instant reality.

Having had a long bath, she emerged an hour and a half later to the sound of voices emanating from one of the many reception rooms. Caught in the weird situation of having been intimate with a man, and yet ignorant of a huge tranche of his life, Holly was uncomfortable with the notion of making herself at home. Somehow it didn't feel right just to breeze into his kitchen—which wasn't the kitchen she had disingenuously assumed he would have but a masterpiece of high-tech modernism—in order to make a cup of coffee, using a machine which looked as though it would require a degree in engineering to master it.

Nor would she have felt comfortable settling in one of the sofas and switching on the television—if there even *was* a television concealed somewhere in the sitting room. At any rate, there was no time for watching telly. She had to talk to him, clarify exactly what was going on. She followed the sound of the voices which led her to the enormous conservatory at the back of the house and a sight that made her mouth fall open inelegantly.

Sprawled on one of the chairs, Luiz was absently switching his attention between his laptop, which lay open on a small glass table next to him, and two women who were busily unpacking several boxes and carrier bags stuffed with clothes. He looked up as soon as Holly appeared.

'What's going on?' Holly asked faintly.

'Holiday clothes.' He gestured nonchalantly to the women who had looked up to shoot her quick, curious smiles before returning to what they had been doing. 'You can't go shopping, so the shopping has come to you.' He hadn't been able to buy her anything when they had been lovers. Having written himself into the role of Mr Average, his generosity had hit a brick wall. Now, and for the first time in living memory, he had rather enjoyed personally having a hand in a shopping spree. He frowned at the perplexed, disapproving expression on her face.

'Luiz, I have no idea what you're talking about. I don't want any of this stuff. I've packed clothes…'

Luiz wondered when he was going to hear some form of gratitude from her. Was it just her pride talking or was his show of wealth really such a big turn-off for her? He decided to go with the pride. Anything else would open the door to disturbing thoughts that she really and truly didn't like the man she now thought he was, which in turn would bring him back to the mythical soul mate lurking round the corner.

'Where we're going will be warm,' he said bluntly, while indicating the chair next to him. 'You probably won't fit into your summer clothes from last year, if you even thought to bring any.'

Holly's eyes flickered to the two women, who were discreet enough to be making a very big show of being deaf.

She didn't want to cause a scene but more than anything else she wanted to tell him that this wasn't her thing at all.

'I've brought all my larger-fitting clothes,' she breathed *sotto voce* as she flopped into the chair indicated. 'Where are we going? Do I have to try all that stuff on?'

'Weirdly, most women would be thrilled to have all this brought to their door,' Luiz remarked drily.

'I'm not most women.'

'More and more I see that as the understatement of the decade and, yes, trying on might be an idea. So…' He leaned back and stretched out his long legs and lightly linked his fingers on his lap. 'What about a catwalk?'

'You're kidding!'

'There's no need to look so horrified. If memory serves me, you used to enjoy strutting your stuff for me…'

A wash of colour flooded Holly's face. In a heartbeat, she was remembering last winter, when the snow had been falling outside and, giggling and slightly tipsy, she had given him his own private striptease in front of the roaring open fire while he had relaxed, pretty much as he was doing now, his lazy, sexy eyes hungrily appreciating the curves on offer.

'There's no point talking about the past,' she said stiffly.

'Nor is there any point pretending that it didn't exist.' He waved the two girls over and informed them that they could go. 'What's not taken will be returned. Tell Bob Harvey to make sure you both get generous tips for your service.' The second they had left the room, he turned to her. 'Stop trying to play this game of disconnect. And stop shooting me down every time I try and ease the situation.'

'That's not fair.'

'It may not be fair but it's the truth. Now, are you going to try those clothes on? Pick whatever you want, and please don't engineer an argument on the difficulties of accepting anything from me. We've entered a new phase of our relationship and you'll just have to get with the programme.'

Holly swallowed hard. She didn't want to argue with him all the time. She knew it was pointless. Plus it made her feel on edge and at odds with herself. She was just not accustomed to arguing with him, yet there was safety in arguments because they helped her widen the distance between them.

She stood up and took a few tentative steps towards the array of rainbow-coloured clothes on the backs of chairs, still neatly folded in boxes, hanging on the makeshift clothes-rail that had been brought with them. She glanced over her shoulder. 'I look terrible in bright colours.' But the silk, cotton and jersey under her fingers were seductive. 'And I'm not parading in front of you,' she warned. 'I'm fat. Much fatter than I was…'

'You're pregnant. Pregnant is sexy.'

Holly tried her best to ignore that throwaway observation. She would bet her house that he had never uttered those words in his life before, and she was uneasily aware of just how much he was willing to accommodate for the sake of doing what he thought was best, right down to saying what he thought she wanted to hear in an attempt to relax her. Was it any wonder that she got on his nerves with her stubborn refusal to play along?

Well, she would bite back any retorts and go along with this trying-on charade. Reluctantly, she gathered up a handful of clothes and headed for the partition which had been erected at the end of the conservatory. It made a spacious and private changing room. When she tentatively peeked her head round, it was to see Luiz absorbed in whatever work he was doing on his computer. He might be there in body, but he certainly was not there in mind.

She remembered a handful of occasions when he had displayed that trait, that immense capacity for losing himself in work to the exclusion of everything around him. She had teased him that they should pay him more for having to slave over a computer on a weekend. It struck her that *that* had certainly not changed. He had always been single-mindedly focused and he still was.

More relaxed, knowing that he wasn't waiting behind that partition trying to coerce her into coming out, Holly began to enjoy the process of trying on the clothes. She dragged the box over, along with some of the dresses draped on the backs of the chairs, and was rewarded with a brief, abstracted glance from Luiz.

Much as she hated to admit it, she never realised that trying on clothes could be so much fun. In fact, confronted with so much choice, she was finding it next to impossible to select items.

Nor did she look as appalling as she had feared. In fact, the colours suited her. Terracottas, oranges, greens and shades of gold all seemed to bring out the best in her complexion. Had he deliberately hand-chosen those colours? How had he managed to do so well in guessing her size? Everything was loose, but everything she tried on seemed to fit just right. He must have been very specific in his requests. Just thinking that he might have actually gone to a great deal of trouble on her behalf gave her a rush of delighted pleasure which she did her best to stifle.

Unfortunately, having gone to the effort, he had clearly lost interest. Piqued, Holly stepped out from behind the partition. The sundress was wonderfully accommodating for her gently expanding stomach, yet attractive, colourful and very fashionable.

'What do you think?' She told herself that this was normal behaviour; shying away and jumping every time he got within five feet of her was not. She gave a little twirl.

Having taken refuge behind his computer in a vain attempt to block out images of Holly getting undressed behind the partition, Luiz looked up. There was no hiding the fact of her pregnancy in the light summer dress, and he had never seen anything so sexy before. The force of his reaction stunned him, because since when had he ever been the kiddy type who waxed lyrical about pregnancy being sexy? True, there was virile satisfaction to be had from the fact that his baby was growing in her stomach, but her fecund body was the most potent aphrodisiac he could ever have imagined. Was she aware of how sheer the dress was? Or perhaps it was the light in the conservatory that made it possible for him to see everything underneath the fine fabric.

She must have removed her bra to try on the selection of swimsuits he had ordered. He could see the perfect shape of her breasts. He could almost make out the dark circles of her nipples.

'I can't see properly when you're standing so far away.' He snapped shut his laptop and straightened in the chair. 'Walk towards me.'

'I told you that I wasn't going to parade…' But, Lord, how she missed being the centre of his attention. She sashayed towards him. The dress was so soft and silky and it felt so cool and sexy brushing against her skin.

'There's a difference between walking and parading,' Luiz murmured. And she definitely was parading.

'Well? What do you think?'

'Nice colours.'

*Nice colours?* Didn't he know that she was asking for something a little more personal than *nice colours?* For a few wild seconds, she was back to that place in time when she just wanted to see that tell-tale flare of desire in his eyes. The force of her craving left her shaken.

'But how do you think it looks on me?' she persisted. She shouldn't care whether he said something flattering or not, but his lack of reaction made her wonder if her pregnant body was a turn-off, despite what he had said earlier about pregnancy being sexy. Of course he was going to say that pregnancy was sexy! He was making a point of not arguing with her. He was determined to be the good guy, doing 'the right thing'! Notably he hadn't said that *she* was a sexy pregnant woman!

'It looks…very fetching.' Luiz stood up and walked towards her with his hands in his pockets. He circled her slowly, as if he was a fashion designer inspecting his product. He stood back, head to one side, rocking on the balls of his feet, and surveyed her from top to bottom.

'You mean *the colours are nice…*'

'Are you fishing for compliments?' He liked the thought of that.

'Of course not!' Holly said loftily. 'I just don't want to make a fool of myself wearing something that's not appropriate given my…shape and size. I've never liked those girls who think that they can just carry on dressing in normal clothes and ignoring the fact that they've got a great big bulge sticking out in front of them. There's no way I would wear jeans and a cropped top and leave my stomach out there for the whole world to see.'

'Nor would I allow you to do that.' If anyone saw her pregnant stomach, it would be him. He had walked away from her—admittedly with a certain amount of reluctance—because he had known that theirs was a relationship that was going nowhere. However, the fierce possessiveness that made him see red at the thought of any other man ogling her lush body was confusing. Had the very fact of her pregnancy brought out a side to him that he hadn't known existed? Certainly that seemed to be the case. 'The dress is entirely appropriate, although…'

'Although…?'

'It seems to be quite sheer.'

'What do you mean *sheer?*'

'Transparent. To put it bluntly, I can see that you're not wearing a bra.'

Holly went bright red. She resisted the urge to stick her hands over her breasts. The saying about the stable door shutting after the horse had bolted came to mind. He had seen her naked a thousand times before. It would be ridiculous to suddenly start reacting to what he had said with maidenly outrage.

'I took it off because I was trying on swimsuits.'

'Guessed as much. You must have gone up a bra size. Did the swimsuits fit?' She would be a lot more than a handful now and he itched to discover for himself exactly how much more.

'They're stretchy. You still haven't told me where we're going, aside from it's going to be hot.' She tried to ignore the way her breasts were tingling and her nipples were tight and sensitive. It was as if his proximity generated an automatic response in her body over which she had no control. She wanted to feel his big hands cupping her breasts… She wanted to luxuriate in the sensation of his mouth covering one of her big, ripe nipples while he teased it with his tongue. Her eyelids fluttered and she knew that her breathing was soft and uneven.

'So the swimsuits fit—that's good. You should have shown me; I could have given my impartial opinion.' God, he could *smell* her desire. As always it matched his, but there was no way he was going to make a move on her. Still, he was hard and fiercely aroused. In fact, it took sheer willpower to remain this close to her without touching.

'I told you that I wasn't going to parade in front of you.'

'Because you feel…fat? Self-conscious? You shouldn't,' he said roughly. 'Pregnancy suits you.'

'You're just saying that.' Holly knew that this conversation was dangerous. She should be walking away and smartly gathering up what she had decided to take. She should be crisply asking for details of the trip ahead and parroting back to him what he had told her earlier about them entering a new phase in their relationship. Instead, she was dithering in front of him, mesmerised by his dark eyes and the soft, velvety drawl of his voice.

'Am I?'

Holly was horrified when of its own accord, her hand reached out and touched his chest. It was like touching a live electric current.

'No touching,' Luiz murmured. 'Your rules, I believe?'

'I wasn't…' She withdrew her hand, mortified, and glared up at him.

'Yes, you were. You don't have to be ashamed of the fact that you still want me.'

'I don't want to have this conversation. I *don't* want you. You're not the person I thought you were! Why would I still want you?'

'Because you're attracted to me and it cuts through all the reasons you keep finding for denying it. Let's face it—if I wanted, I could have you right here, right now, surrounded by clothes, on the rug, damn the consequences…'

Holly tottered a few steps back. He was right and she hated herself for being so weak and pathetic. How could she still be so consumed by a man who had used her? Who had never seen her as a long-term partner? Who was only with her now because of her situation? Was she so lacking in self-respect?

'Okay,' she admitted tersely. 'So you still turn me on.'

'And at last you're admitting it. Honesty is always the best policy.'

'It's just a physical thing,' she muttered fiercely. 'It's just a left-over reaction from what we had. It doesn't mean anything!' She turned away abruptly. Her eyes stung with angry unshed tears. She thought she could detect smug satisfaction in his voice. So she had refused to marry him. Did he imagine that she was still so besotted with him that she would continue having sex with him?

Another, darker thought infiltrated her brain. He had meant it when he had said that he wouldn't tolerate another man bringing up his child. Knowing him as well as she did, she didn't doubt that for a second. Did he think that he could use her continuing attraction to him as a way of keeping her tethered to him? With no marriage, he would be free to cast his net somewhere else, yet he would continue to command her loyalty because she couldn't fight the dictates of her own weak, cowardly body.

Was Luiz Casella a man who seriously thought that he could have his cake and eat it, and was she so stupid that she would allow him to get away with it? She would just have to try harder to steel herself against the physical impact he still had on her. Deprived of essential nutrients, lust was something fragile that would wither away in no time at all.

'You still haven't given me any details about this trip.' She kept her face a perfect blank as she looked up at him, arms folded.

'Sit. Good. Okay, I have an ongoing project—one of the Bermudian islands—an eco-hotel catering for the discerning client. It's to be the first of several across the world.'

'You're into hotels?' Holly was distracted enough to ask. 'But I thought you were into computers.'

'In business, it makes sense not to put all your eggs in one basket.'

'So we're going to…to the Caribbean?'

'I wouldn't let any of the locals hear you say that,' Luiz told her with a wry smile. 'The climate may be great, but technically it's closer to New York as the crow flies. My family has had a house there for many years so I know the islands quite well. They've got their downsides; possibly a little too wet for some tourists, and a little too cool at certain times of the year for the dedicated sunbather, but they're paradise for anyone with a love of nature.'

Holly was thinking how, in a few words, he had encapsulated all the differences between them.

'I've been abroad twice in my entire life,' she told him flatly. 'Once with my dad to Marbella and once on a school trip to Normandy.'

'So this should make a pleasant change of scenery,' Luiz inserted smoothly. 'I had a planned trip out there to check up on a few details, make sure things are running smoothly. Made sense to bring it forward in light of recent events.'

'So it would be something of a working holiday for you…' Holly said slowly, liking the sound of that. 'How long would we be over there for?'

'A couple of weeks.'

'And your empire could do without you for such a long time?'

'My empire will be fine without me.'

'Well, I've made two separate piles of clothes. I don't like accepting anything from you…'

'That's a given. But…?'

'But I've chosen some stuff. Not much.'

Luiz looked at her heightened colour. He believed her when she said that she hadn't chosen much. Any other woman would have greedily taken everything on offer.

'Look, Luiz…' Holly cleared her throat awkwardly. 'What happened just then…we have a certain amount of history. Of course, I'm still, well, let's just say that when a person breaks up it takes a while to recover. When my ex and I…'

'Not interested.'

'What do you mean?'

'We don't need to put on old records and replay the past. I don't want to hear about the lingering effects of your break-up with your ex.' Nor did he want to get into a self-delusional conversation in which she would subtly try to imply that she wasn't attracted to him.

'You really don't have a sentimental bone in your body, do you?'

'None that I have ever noticed,' Luiz said coolly. And yet, there had been times after he had left her when the emptiness of his bed had struck something at the very core of him, when the snatch of some silly pop song on the radio had made him switch channels. Had those unconscious signals prompted him to consider Cecelia as marriage material in an attempt to shut the door on Holly whom he had privately seen as unfinished business? Did the mind operate in ways like that? Luiz had always prided himself on a straightfor-ward approach to all issues emotional. Emotions existed, reasons for behaviour existed, but analysing any of that stuff just wasn't for him. He left that to people with time on their hands and nothing much productive to do with it. So to find himself going down an introspective path was frustrating and he stamped down any inclination to pursue it.

'Do we leave tomorrow?'

'First thing.' He told her about the flight, the times, the connections. For Holly, she could see why he had chosen to bring his trip forward. The island would be impossible to access for any curious reporter. It was as good as it got in terms of privacy.

From her point of view, the thought of him working was good. It helped to remove the nagging sense of guilt that he was prepared to rise to the occasion and alter his tailor-made life in whatever way was necessary, while she stood on the sidelines quibbling and finding reasons to knock him back so that she could tenaciously cling to what she knew. Also, a hotel was good. A hotel implied a certain amount of detachment. She would be able to lose herself amongst other people.

He had told her that he needed to see how things were progressing and she assumed he meant having a look at the books, making sure that a healthy profit was being made. She was under no illusion that whatever he chose to do would be successful. It dawned on her that she had had that opinion of him even when they had been involved with one another. True, then her ideas had been woolly assumptions, but they had still been here. Reality had only confirmed her own impressions.

So, while he checked the profit and loss columns and closeted himself away in meetings with the finance department, she would be able to lose herself in the crowds. All said and done, her experience of foreign destinations was lamentably non-existent. She felt a stirring of excitement.

She switched off as he told her about the technicalities of the trip, reassuring her that his people could sort out all the necessary details. She was vaguely aware of him filling in a few blanks about the various islands, the population, the scenery. Her mind was miles away. She wished she had had some warning of their destination. She would have liked to buy a guide book. Then she guiltily thought that she could hardly be sniffy about accepting some clothes from him whilst bristling with excitement at the prospect of enjoying an all-expenses-paid holiday in the sun. She surfaced to find him looking at her with raised eyebrows.

'Okay. So I haven't been away for a long time. It's been hard to find the time to leave the sanctuary.'

'There is a stack of guide books and history books in the office. Some of them are dated but some are pretty up to date, bought by my people when they were scouting for a suitable spot for the hotel. Feel free to avail yourself of them.'

'How did you know what I was thinking?' Holly demanded and she was knocked sideways by the smile he gave her. It was just one of those amused, complicit smiles that had always made her toes curl and her tummy turn to liquid. She fought to hang on to the new relationship they now had. It seemed a good time to lay down a few ground rules, as much for herself as anything else.

'When did I ever not know what you were thinking?'

That struck an unpleasant chord with Holly. While she had been transparent as glass, he had been as opaque as fog and clever at hiding it.

'Why did I never realise that that would end up being a bad thing?' she said in a rueful murmur. She looked at him, clear eyed and determined.

'Come again?'

'It doesn't matter. I just think that now's a good time to have a chat about…about what happens when we get there.'

'Chat away!' Luiz settled himself more comfortably in the chair and looked at her in expectant silence.

'I know you don't like discussing feelings, Luiz. Feelings don't always come in a neat little box that you can work out and make sense of…'

'Thank you for that, but what's the point you're getting at?'

'I still have feelings for you. *Not,*' she hastened to tack on, 'on the emotional front but on the physical level. You didn't want me to talk about my ex, so I won't, but I guess I'm still attracted to you, and believe me I don't like myself for it. We wouldn't be in this position now at all if it weren't for that fact that I'm having a baby. In fact, I would have moved on…found myself a new boyfriend.' Even in her wildest imagination, Holly couldn't imagine this as a real possibility.

'The perfect soul mate?' Luiz enquired coldly.

Holly nodded. She wondered what this perfect soul mate

would look like. As it turned out, Luiz Casella was the least perfect man she could ever have fallen in love with, yet everything about him was so big, so vibrantly, sexily overwhelming, that he shoved all other attempts at a comparison out of the picture.

'But it's no point talking about ifs and buts.' She sadly relinquished her attempts to imagine this fictional soul mate which would have made life so much easier. 'If we're going to be stuck with one another for the next couple of weeks, then it's important for you to know that what we have now is just...a working relationship, and I don't want it complicated by...anything.'

Was she giving him a snappy lecture on keeping his hands to himself? Luiz thought with a surge of impotent fury. When she had been the one reaching out to touch him only a short while before? He also didn't care for the term 'stuck with'. It seemed to him that no sooner were they communicating without rancour than she did her best to stir up antipathy. Worse was the knowledge that this was something she was doing almost unconsciously. Dragged along in the wake of unexpected events, Luiz was bewildered and impatient with himself for not being the one to control the outcome. Any headway he made slithered through his fingers like water.

'Are you addressing me when you say that or yourself?' he drawled, watching with scrupulous concentration as she blushed.

'Both of us! I just feel that we mustn't let...let anything get in the way of us just being friends.'

'Then make sure you don't touch me because I don't have any scruples on that front at all.'

'You don't mean that. You said that we were entering a new phase in our relationship!'

'That would be the phase where you start realising that

you don't have an option but to accept my generosity. As far as sex is concerned, I'm not into pretending that I no longer fancy you. I do.'

'You can't. You found yourself a girlfriend! How could you fancy her and then suddenly fancy me?' Holly didn't care whether she sounded bitter and jealous.

'So I didn't fancy Cecelia.' Luiz shrugged. The admission was grudgingly imparted and he flushed darkly at this concession, which went against the grain.

'You didn't? Are you telling me that you never slept with her?'

'Why are we focusing on this?' Luiz looked at her with brooding force, challenging her to pursue a topic he no longer wanted to discuss, and Holly was happy to give way. All she could think was…*Luiz had never made love to Cecelia.* She took that to mean that he had remained faithful to her whilst they had been apart. Okay, so it wasn't a huge deal, she told herself. But she couldn't clear her mind of the uplifting notion that, whether he admitted it or not, she had meant more to him than he had been prepared to say.

Reality slowly dripped in as she acknowledged the other side of the coin which was that, whilst he hadn't dumped her and instantly jumped into the sack with someone else, she was being shown that he was capable of indulging in a relationship that had a future without sex being the primary impetus. This was a lesson in how far his head ruled his emotions, except in the case of Cecelia his head hadn't been forced kicking and screaming into submission. Cecelia had been his Plan A and, sadly for him, he had been pushed into a Plan B he hadn't banked on. Suddenly, whether he had been attracted to Cecelia or not seemed a very insignificant detail barely worth getting all worked up about.

'We're not,' Holly returned tightly.

'Good, because it's irrelevant.' He was disturbed by her

lack of reaction to his confession that he hadn't fancied Cecelia. He realised that he had expected her to jump for joy. Once again, he realised how much his predictions of her behaviour were based on past patterns that were no longer applicable. 'If you want to keep us on a friends-only basis, then that's fine. I won't make a move on you. I'll be the perfect gentleman. But if you come close, then on your own head be it, because I'm not in the market for allocating Brownie points to myself for self-denial.'

'If you're referring to that incident earlier, it won't happen again!' She would make sure that she was never alone with him. That could work. They would be in a hotel. Tourists would be lounging around sipping cocktails and getting burnt. It would be easy to keep everything polite and businesslike with a bunch of strangers around as unwitting chaperones to their every conversation.

'As long as we have clarity on the subject,' he drawled. 'Now, if you put aside what you've decided to take with you, then I'll bring it all upstairs and you can pack. Your suitcase won't hold everything. I will ensure that you have more.'

'And do you think that we'll be bugged by reporters?' She had completely forgotten the reason for her presence in his house and the necessity for going abroad. In Luiz's presence, everything flew out of her head. He just had that effect on her.

'Nothing I won't be able to manage. I'm going to have to devote the rest of the day to work, but feel free to relax wherever you want. I've made sure that there's ample food in the house. Help yourself.'

Holly had no idea how he expected her to relax. When he said that he was going to have to work, did he mean that he would be out of the house? She guessed that he would have to pack in as much as he could before he disappeared on a trip across the Atlantic, and once again she was uncomfortably aware of how much he was sacrificing.

'What would you do if I lost the baby?' she asked.

In the process of standing, Luiz stilled and stared down at her upturned face. 'Is there something you should be telling me?'

'No,' Holly sighed. 'I just…wondered.'

'I don't deal in hypotheses.' His answer was sharper than he had intended, but what a question! He had been momentarily poleaxed by the crazy notion that the path he was on was not altogether disagreeable. In fact… 'And you shouldn't, either.' He moderated his tone and dispelled the conflicting emotions her question had engendered. 'It doesn't do anyone any good.'

'You're so pragmatic, Luiz.' But she smiled tiredly at him.

'You have shadows under your eyes,' he remarked roughly.

'Things have been a bit stressful recently.'

Luiz raked his fingers through his hair. 'If I've given you a hard time, I apologise.'

Holly's eyes widened in surprise. 'You haven't,' she mumbled awkwardly. She was much more efficient at giving herself a hard time than he could ever be. She fought and struggled and waged a ceaseless internal war and it wasn't going to get her anywhere. They were on opposite sides of an enormous wall and that wasn't going to change. He could give her so much, but he couldn't give her what she really wanted and that wasn't his fault. Wasn't it about time she stopped punishing them both for something he just couldn't help? He didn't love her and springing attacks on him wasn't going to change that unalterable truth.

She held out her hand and smiled. 'Friends, Luiz?'

A brief hesitation and then he clasped her hand. 'Friends,' he agreed.

# CHAPTER EIGHT

HOLLY'S PLAN TO play it cool was demolished the minute she reached the airport and discovered that they were flying first-class. She had left Luiz in peace whilst they had been chauffeured to the airport, choosing instead to gaze out of the window and feverishly speculate on what the next fortnight would bring. She had ignored him when, stepping out of the sleek, black car, he had immediately taken a phone call and had remained on the phone for the next fifteen minutes. He checked them in with the ease of the seasoned traveller, barely noticing the goggling check-in girl in the smart uniform as he continued his phone call, hardly glancing up.

She had nodded when he had informed her that there would be no time to shop in the duty free because he needed to get to the lounge so that he could access reports on his computer—and, besides, hadn't she always told him that she hated shopping? All told they had exchanged a mere handful of words since leaving the house, although he had made sure that she ate far more breakfast than she intended to, standing over her like a sergeant major, lecturing her on the importance of good nutrition during pregnancy.

Never having considered the prospect of fatherhood, he seemed to have enmeshed himself in it with wholehearted fervour, but then Luiz had never been one to do anything by halves. Fix one section of the fence and the entire fence had to undergo an overhaul. The single meal he had ever cooked for her had turned into a production with half the local market being bought and enough steak to open a small shop.

Now, as he hurried her through the main terminal, she lost herself in the grim reality of Luiz flinging himself into the role of friend. He would speak to her with casual, studied politeness and he would make sure she looked after herself for just as long as it took for his child to be born, and then they would develop an amicable but distant relationship, only ever discussing stuff to do with their child. Whatever attraction he still had for her would fizzle out and he would become involved with another Cecelia in due course.

As was her habit, Holly became fully engaged in her mental scenario and only surfaced when she realised that they had left the busy main drag of the terminal behind and had entered a private lounge, stuffed with comfy chairs, sofas and little secluded kiosks for private office work. There was a central area, shiny and laden with every description of pastry; there were jugs of juice, bottles of wine and champagne and a dining area with full waiter service.

Holly stopped dead in her tracks and stared.

In the process of scrolling through his phone to pick up emails, Luiz only realised he had left her behind after a couple of seconds and then he spun round on his heels, amused to see her staring round her with a shell-shocked expression.

'I never knew places like this existed,' Holly breathed, impressed.

'Welcome to the world of the über-rich.' He grinned and led her towards one of the sofas. 'What would you like to drink?' He gestured to the bar area. 'There's pretty much everything you could possibly want on offer, including hard spirits for the traveller who doesn't really care how much of a nuisance he makes of himself on a plane...'

Holly laughed and Luiz realised how much he had missed

the sound of her carefree laughter. She used to laugh a lot when they had been together. Ever since she had returned to his life, the laughter had been conspicuously absent. He strove not to dwell on the perfectly reasonable gripe that there were little grounds for her continual wary suspicion of him, her constant lack of enthusiasm for falling in, her semi-permanent sniper attacks when he had gone way beyond the extra mile. It seemed that it was impossible for her to get past what had happened between them but he wasn't going to focus on that because, as far as he was concerned, there was no point.

'The stories I could tell…' he murmured, with a crooked smile. He liked the fact that she was relaxing. He wondered whether this was because she no longer felt threatened by him now that they were *friends*. The grin on his face remained but felt slightly more strained. 'On one memorable flight, the plane had to make an emergency landing back at Heathrow because one of the guys in first class had overdone it on the alcohol and got it into his head that he wanted to find out what being a terrorist might be like.'

'You're kidding. A businessman?'

'Pop star.'

'You never told me that story before.'

'I wasn't a billionaire who took first-class flights at the time.'

The hurt lying just below the surface threatened to spill over but Holly smiled bravely through it and was proud of her adult reaction which so exactly mirrored his. 'I'm surprised you weren't bored stiff visiting me on weekends,' she said truthfully, before remembering that his visits had all been about sex and therefore would have enabled him to ride the boredom he surely would have felt helping out with the animals and in winter and doing DIY jobs around the sanctuary. In his real life, he would have been able to snap his fingers and have an army of minions steaming in to fix whatever needed fixing. Actually, in real life, he probably didn't get near any animals, never mind a motley assortment of discarded or abused ones.

'Why would I have been?'

'You have everything you want in London. Flash cars, big house, first-class travel… I bet you eat out all the time in fancy restaurants.'

Luiz was tempted to tell her that variety was the spice of life but he knew that she would find that observation offensive. He also knew that it barely skimmed the surface of why she had been his longest lasting lover. 'I don't do much home cooking,' he conceded, keeping it light.

'Even though you have a fantastic kitchen.'

'You noticed.'

'I had a look around when I arrived before you got back. I hope you don't mind.'

Luiz squashed the surge of irritation and impatience at her token politeness. Hell, he almost preferred it when she was spoiling for a fight. 'Why would I?'

Holly shrugged. 'Your house is so pristine,' she admitted. 'I mean, it's beautiful but it doesn't look as though it's lived in. I didn't want to mess anything up.'

'Oh, for God's sake!' Luiz flung his arms wide in an expressive gesture of impatience. 'Do you really think I would give a damn if you spilled something on the sofa or trailed muddy footprints on the rug?'

'I don't know, Luiz. Would you?'

'One step forward, two steps back. Are you making it your mission to get on my nerves? Hell. Forget I said that. I'll go get us something to drink. Want a newspaper?'

'I've got the guide books.' She almost said *and I hope you don't mind; I'll make sure to return them…*

The thought of being friends with Luiz was as daunting

a prospect as a walk up Mount Everest in flip flops. Bitterness lay in wait, ready to ambush every innocent remark and inoffensive question. Was it any wonder that he was tiring of her?

Awkward silence greeted his return and he made no move to forward the conversation. In fact, he excused himself and retreated to one of the private kiosks where, out of the corner of her eye, she saw him alternately on the phone and on his computer.

By the time the flight was called, Holly was fully up to date on quite a lot factual information abut their destination. The entire plane had been boarded aside from the handful of first-class passengers who had been called last, and thereby rewarded with the privilege of being able to stroll into their seats, bypassing all crowds.

She made sure not to comment on the luxury of the first-class cabin into which they were ushered. He took all this for granted. He didn't look around him. He barely glanced at the flight attendant offering them champagne, which he waved aside. 'Not brilliant for jet lag.' He settled into his seat and glanced at Holly. 'Talk to me. You've barely muttered a word since we left the house, aside from your contentious remarks about my house.'

'That's because I didn't want to disturb you.'

'Since when did you ever mind disturbing me? And please don't tell me that I've suddenly become a stranger you have to tiptoe around who lives in a show home you're scared of getting dirty.'

'What do you want me to talk about?'

'Anything and everything.'

'I'm not a wind-up puppet.' Talking had never been a problem when they had been together. In fact, she had used to stockpile little bits and pieces of things that had happened during the week so that she could tell him when she saw him at the weekends. 'Do you still think that I'm a potential gold-digger after your money now that I've discovered how much of it you've got?' she asked bluntly.

Luiz looked at her carefully. 'I judged you once. It was a mistake and I shouldn't have,' he told her. 'Another way of looking at things is to realise that we would never have gone out had you met me under normal circumstances. That's the inescapable truth. The very fact that I was Luiz Gomez and not Luiz Casella ensured a much longer relationship than any of the previous relationships I've had with women in the past.'

'And it honestly didn't bother you that I might have wanted more out of the relationship than you were ever going to be prepared to give?'

'How was I to predict that you would suddenly decide to start talking about a future?' Luiz frowned because he should have known. She had not been like one of the high-maintenance glamorous models he usually dated, easily pleased with expensive trinkets and easily discarded without a backward glance.

'Didn't your previous girlfriends ever want more than just sex?'

'When I said talk to me, this wasn't quite the conversation I had been expecting.'

'Friends are open and honest with one another,' Holly inserted lightly. Just saying that felt like swallowing glass. So he had selfishly floated along on a tide of uncomplicated, freely given sex and easy companionship from someone who never asked for anything, not even for a show of commitment. 'I'm trying to put everything into perspective.'

'And what's the practical upside of that in terms of your pregnancy?'

Holly shrugged and lowered her eyes. 'You never answered my question about your girlfriends... Did you dump them when they started talking about a long-term relationship?'

'I never allowed things to get to that point,' Luiz grudgingly conceded. He hadn't cared for the whole 'honesty between friends' bandwagon she now appeared to be on nor was he impressed by her polite monotone. He dearly wanted to tell her that the 'friends' lark was going to prove highly challenging when the air between them sizzled with sexual electricity. So she wanted her space, and he was going to give it to her, but he was already getting restless. He didn't like the fact that nothing had been sorted out between them. Patience had never been one of his virtues.

'So you used them, and then tossed them aside when you were finished with them, before they could start asking awkward questions.'

'Why do you have to be so dramatic?'

Holly reddened because his voice was amused and teasing. And he was so close to her. She could see the length of his lashes and the hint of gold flecks in the dark eyes. He had rid himself of his jacket and was wearing a black polo shirt which exposed his strong forearms which she had always found outrageously masculine. She could feel her heart pick up speed and her mouth went dry. It was blessed relief when the plane began to taxi.

She had already checked in twice with Andy to find out how everything was going. Now her phone was switched off and she felt excitement unfurl inside her.

When she closed her eyes, it was easy to wipe away the past few weeks and pretend that this was the holiday with him she had longed for. Of course, in her dreams they had been flying somewhere cheap and sitting at the back of the plane. Her stomach lurched as the plane accelerated sharply upwards and she was only aware of her clenched fists when Luiz gently prised her fingers apart and linked them with his.

'You're tense,' he murmured. 'Relax.' He absently stroked her thumb with his finger which practically deprived her of the power of breathing.

'I haven't been on a plane for a long time,' Holly muttered tightly. 'I'd forgotten how much I hated taking off.'

'Just distract yourself by thinking about something else.' He continued to stroke her thumb even though he knew that just that fleeting feel of her satin-smooth skin under his finger was turning him on. 'Think about me,' he encouraged softly. 'You were telling me what a monster I was for leading poor innocent girls up the garden path before cruelly getting rid of them just when they least expect it.'

The way he said that drew any possible sting out of whatever she had been going to say. His lazy tone of self-irony invited her to laugh. Holly smiled without meeting his eyes, very conscious of that gentle pressure on her thumb whilst pretending that nothing was happening.

'Except that, in my defence, I've never made promises I couldn't keep,' he murmured and Holly opened her eyes and looked at him. She wondered whether this was his way of telling her that she had read way too much into their relationship. So he hadn't spelt it out in words of one syllable that he wasn't in it for the long haul, but he had never promised her anything. Unlike the rest of the women he had dated in the past, however, she had failed to take the hint. She had innocently taken him at face value and assumed that he was putting in as much as she had been. That would be the danger of going out with a country bumpkin, as he had discovered to his cost: too dim-witted to read the writing on the wall.

She wriggled her fingers free and reached for her capacious handbag into which she had stuffed all the guide books.

'Tell me about your hotel,' she asked, changing the subject.

'Eventually it's not going to work, you know.'

'What isn't going to work?'

'I mean, if you want me to talk about my hotel, then I'm happy to oblige but sooner or later we're going to have to really talk about what happens next.'

'We've already talked about that. I've already told you that I'm not prepared to become someone you're saddled with. I've already said that we both deserve better.'

'Actually, moving on from the marriage scenario,' Luiz said smoothly, 'I was talking about the financial arrangements that will have to be put in place.'

'Oh.' So he had actually listened to what she had said and had dropped the crazy idea that they should get married for the sake of a baby. She had thought that she might have to really do battle with a wall of stubborn refusal to see the light and she decided that she surely must be happy and relieved at his decision.

'Money-wise, I will ensure that you receive a healthy monthly allowance from me to cover your needs and the needs of our child.'

Holly was examining how it was that she felt less radiantly happy than she should at the notion that he had dropped all talk of trying to force her into a marriage she didn't want.

'It's up to you whether we involve a lawyer in this arrangement. I would suggest we do; it will make everything cleaner and more straightforward.'

She realised how difficult it was going to prove in dealing with him like a business acquaintance and treating something as intimate as a child as though it were a transaction to be dealt with efficiently and dispassionately.

'Naturally, I will also set up a trust fund for our child and a separate bank account for any expenses you might think you need that fall outside the normal domain. You will find my generosity beyond reproach.'

'Oh, yes, the money thing…' Holly said vaguely.

'Have you been listening to a word I've been saying?' If she had wanted to display just how little she thought of his wealth, then she couldn't have picked a better way of doing it because she was staring at him with a glazed expression that said it all.

'Of course I have. I know you'll be a good provider, Luiz.'

'Good,' he said flatly. 'Which brings me to the next problem.'

'Which is what?' She wished he would stop seeing things in terms of problems that had to be sorted and technicalities that had to be wrapped up, yet how could she blame him?

'The problem of the commute.'

'I've been giving that some thought,' Holly told him. 'And I know that it's only fair that I compromise on the issue of where we live. By *we*...' she stressed, just in case he thought that she was too thick to get the message that he had dropped the marriage angle, 'I mean me and the baby.'

'Of course.' An element of cool had crept into his voice. Had he thought that underneath the 'friends only' clause lurked the barely recognised notion that she would come to her senses? Had he agreed to play along with her terms and conditions because he retained the confidence that she would eventually climb out of her shell-shocked reaction to his perfectly understandable lie and come round to his point of view? He always got his own way. He had spoken to his mother and had successfully evaded the whole question of marriage whilst still managing to imply that naturally it would happen. He had taken a back step and held off returning to the subject; what if it was actually a subject to which there was no return? Had he really seriously considered that possibility?

'I'm prepared to move further south. Andy says that it should be possible to sell the cottage, along with the grounds and the sanctuary, as a going concern. Of course, I would only sell to the right person. And I wouldn't want to live in London. You mentioned that you would be prepared to travel out for…to…'

Yes, he really *had* assumed that she would see the sense of marrying him. He was now strangely bewildered by her determination to forge ahead and erase him out of her life in all respects aside from the obvious.

'Further south.'

'Somewhere outside London. Easy for you to get to.' Holly imagined him waving goodbye to the latest woman in his life before setting off on a duty trip to see his child. She had seen Cecelia. Whatever he said, she would never be able to compete with any woman he chose to go out with. With appalling clarity she pictured herself as the rotund ex, unable to shift the baby fat and too run off her feet to change out of her unglamorous, comfy clothes liberally stained with baby food as she opened the door to him.

'I would want to carry on doing something,' she continued, still wrapped up in the unflattering image of herself a year down the line.

'But you wouldn't need to,' Luiz was constrained to point out. 'You would never have to work in your life again.'

'And become a kept woman?'

'In my book a kept woman is a woman who comes with benefits.'

'I intend on getting a job just as soon as I can after the baby is born,' Holly stated forcefully. She resentfully wondered what his thoughts on women 'with benefits' would be if he could see her the way she was currently seeing herself, projected in the future, as an overweight, stressed-out frump. Was her determination not to marry him not only linked to the fact that he didn't love her but also to the very real fear that he might one day look at her with contempt and revulsion, should they make the mistake of getting married? A regrettable mistake? An unsophisticated lump who couldn't compete with the skinny models with the shiny hair, tight clothes and the address book packed with the names of celebrity friends?

'A job doing what?' Luiz asked. 'And why would you do anything? I wouldn't want you to… Call me a dinosaur, but as far as I'm concerned the mother of my child should be there to raise him or her.'

'Of course I'll be there!'

'And where would *there* be, actually? A few miles away in an office somewhere? Running errands for some lecherous old guy in his sixties?'

Holly almost burst out laughing. 'Luiz, you really are a dinosaur. Did your mother stay at home to bring you all up?'

'Of course she did.'

'My mum died when I was young. It was just me and my dad.'

'I would have liked your dad,' Luiz muttered. 'He was a traditionalist. Like me.' She had talked about her dad a lot. A warm, funny, kind man. The sort of man who would have frowned on his daughter turning down a marriage proposal. The sort of man who would have encouraged her to see the sense of a child having both parents right there. A man who would have been in his corner. A guy with values in all the right places. Someone who would have had his back…

'He also encouraged me to be independent,' Holly pointed out. 'I didn't have the example of a mother slaving behind a stove while my dad toiled in the fields to bring home the bacon. I was in the fields toiling with my dad.' She sighed. 'I can see why you chose someone like Cecelia,' she said sadly. 'I guess we're all drawn to what we know.'

Luiz gritted his teeth. Hell, how had she managed to do that? He was free-thinking, creative, the sort of guy who could out-think, out-fox and generally get the better of anyone in an argument—yet he seemed to have painted himself into a corner! How the hell had that happened? Somehow she had managed to pigeon-hole him as the sort of buttoned-up, insular, arrogant bore incapable of thinking outside the box.

'Cecelia was a mistake. Been there, got the tee-shirt. Had the conversation. I didn't fancy her.'

'I'm not talking about whether you fancied her or not.' Holly looked at him as though he was on a completely different wavelength. As though he just didn't get it. It should have been a massive turn-off. As a rule women only voiced strident opinions if they thought it might score them Brownie points and turn him on. Those women were few and far between and had never really understood that, for a guy like him, whose daily working life was a combination of stress, pressure and relentless deadlines, the last thing he was looking for was a contrived intellectual challenge. Holly wasn't looking for an intellectual challenge to turn him on or capture his attention. She was simply saying what was on her mind.

'You're not interested in someone with opinions.'

'That's ridiculous. Haven't I supported you with every decision you've ever made?' He glared at her with frustration. 'What about when you wanted to adopt those fifteen geese? Didn't I respect your decision even though I told you you'd live to regret it?' And regret it she had when they had ended up chasing away anyone foolish enough to stop by, terrorising the postman and reducing Buster the donkey to a state of semi-permanent panic attacks in serious need of animal counselling should such a thing have existed.

'You were forced to rehome them.'

Holly counted to ten. How could he not see that his rules were different for a lover? It was easy to patronise someone you didn't care about because it really didn't matter if they disagreed with what you said. But the ground rules changed if you really cared about them. Luiz didn't want the mother of his child to have a job. He might employ his fair share of women but in every other way he was staunchly traditional. Holly had spent nearly two years worshipping the ground he walked on. Now was the time for her to demonstrate some backbone. She would need it. Without it he would trample all over her. He would call the shots.

'And I'm very glad I had them for those eight weeks.'

'Six weeks, three days and four hours. I should know. They were more effective than an alarm clock when it came to getting me out of bed at five-thirty on a Sunday morning.'

Holly's heart skipped a beat. More than anything else, she didn't want to take a trip down memory lane. Memory lane was fraught with danger. Memory lane was filled with picture-postcard perfect recollections of them corralling those geese into the van he had rented for the day, having a pub lunch and splashing out to celebrate with a bottle of cava. Except drinking the cava was extravagant had been a joke given the way reality had unfolded. No; memory lane was definitely a place she didn't want to visit. In short, memory lane was forbidden territory, out of bounds, aggressively guarded with 'no trespassing' signs…

'And that's what it's all about,' she said. 'You may not have fancied Cecelia but she fitted the bill in one really important area—she never questioned you.' Plus she came from the right background, was enough of a trust-fund babe for daddy's cash to make her financially independent, had wanted Luiz for his massive connections and desirable power base but would have been happy never to have questioned his decisions…

'I enjoyed you questioning me!' Luiz didn't care for the box she was trying to stuff him into. When exactly had she become so argumentative? Was it the hormones? Thinking about it, she had never quite slotted into the role of the docile partner. She had always had a point of view.

'I don't think we're getting anywhere with this, Luiz. We're going round in circles.' She breathed in deeply. That baffled, outraged expression on his face. She should have found it infuriating and laughable and she was annoyed with herself for her weak inclination to be indulgent, to idiotically factor in his background and make excuses on his behalf, to accept that he was so much more than the narrow-minded guy she was describing.

Luiz scowled. 'Right. So what's this job you're talking about?'

'I'm not cut out to work in an office,' Holly opined. 'It would drive me mad. I have friends who work in offices; you wouldn't believe the office politics...' She blushed and looked at him with a quick sidelong glance. 'Sorry. Forgot that you work in an office. In my head, you're always on the road trying to sell computers.'

'So, repeat, what job do you have in mind?' Sensing yet another accusatory, reproachful lecture on his deceit, Luiz was keen to steer the conversation into less inflammatory waters.

'I like working with animals,' Holly confessed. 'you know that. But I guess I'd settle for being a receptionist at, say, a vet's.'

'A receptionist.'

'Anyone can answer a phone!'

'You're opinionated. Would you really be able to steer clear of lecturing the woman with the cat that she should have brought it in before its symptoms became too severe?'

'Well, if I can't find a job with an animal sanctuary in the south I'll just have to settle for second best, won't I?'

'Fair enough.' Luiz shrugged.

'And I wouldn't appreciate it if you tried to talk me out of getting a job!'

'I hope I would value my life more than to ever do such a thing.'

'Good!' But she had the unnerving feeling that she might have won the battle but had definitely lost the war. 'So that's all settled. We'll be just another couple bringing up their child as best as they can although they're not living together. No one will care about us. There won't be any scandal and, without a scandal, the paparazzi won't be interested.'

'And what about visiting rights?' Luiz pointed out softly.

'You can visit whenever you want. I would never try and stop you.'

'Surely you would want something in writing? Things might kick off with the optimistic casual assumption that nothing will change, but of course over time things will.'

'What do you mean?'

'Involvement with other people. It happens.'

'I've had enough involvement to last a lifetime.' She couldn't conceal the bitterness that had crept into her voice.

'Bear in mind that perhaps I haven't.'

Holly's heart picked up. She felt her skin prickle with discomfort. Was he simply projecting ahead, looking at a hypothetical future from all angles? He was someone who liked to be prepared, who didn't welcome surprises; she had always known that about him. Or was he already thinking along the traditional lines that if a child needed two parents, and she wasn't prepared to be one married to him, then there was a vacant slot? She went cold at the thought of him arriving to pick up his child in the company of his wife…

'I think it's a bit early to be thinking of stuff like that.'

Luiz shrugged and broke eye contact. 'I like to be prepared for all eventualities. I'll get my lawyer to start working on the details of the arrangement while we're away.'

It all sounded so cold and businesslike, yet what more could she have expected? Why was it that she looked at him and, underneath all the logic and reason, she still yearned for the froth of romance and the joyful optimism of someone with stars in her eyes? How was it that she could carry on loving him despite the fact that she knew she shouldn't? How could she be so lacking in self-esteem that she could still love someone who didn't love her and never would?

'Fine.' She would just have to learn to be more like him, to present a cool, dispassionate veneer, although in her case it would be fake. 'And you never told me about the hotel. Will there be rooms for us? Or is it fully booked? I wouldn't want to put anyone out. I'm happy to have any room in the staff quarters.'

The 'fasten seatbelt' sign had been switched off. In the process of standing up to stretch his muscles, Luiz looked at her with some surprise. 'Firstly, I wouldn't dream of shoving you into staff quarters. You're carrying my child. That fact alone puts you in a completely different category.'

Holly translated that into meaning that she had been upgraded. She was no longer the disposable country-bumpkin girlfriend. What her love and devotion had not been able to achieve, the unplanned baby growing inside her had.

'Secondly, whoever said anything about us staying in the hotel?'

'What do you mean?'

'I mean that it would be difficult to stay in a place which, at the moment, is still in the process of construction. No, we'll be staying at the family house.'

# CHAPTER NINE

HAVING DROPPED THAT bombshell, Luiz had promptly refused her insistence that they discuss what, precisely, he meant by that.

As far as he was concerned, there was nothing to discuss. In response to her outraged shriek, he simply shrugged and glanced at her with raised eyebrows, as though she had taken leave of her senses. He claimed to have no idea where and how she might have arrived at the conclusion that they were going to be staying at the hotel. Hadn't he mentioned that it was work in progress, barely off the starting blocks?

Holly had subjected him to an increasingly virulent attack as the pleasant images of them surrounded by handy tourists disappeared over the horizon. In the end she had flatly stated that there was no way she would be sharing a house with him.

'Why not?' Luiz had looked at her with such genuine curiosity that she had gritted her teeth together and resisted the urge to hit him with one of the guide books in her bag. The heaviest one. 'What's the problem?'

'The problem is that I didn't sign up to sharing a house with you.'

'Repeat—what's the problem?'

Holly realised that he was either incapable of seeing her point of view or else downright refusing to.

'We won't be sharing a bedroom,' Luiz informed her drily, while Holly stubbornly resisted the urge to look away, even though she could feel the tide of embarrassed colour flood her cheeks, because just the thought of being under the same roof as him was debilitating. It was one thing playing the 'just friends' card, but it was quite another to think how strenuously that card would be put to the test when there was just two of them sharing the same space and no longer in their comfort zone.

Naturally, he would not be feeling the same level of hysterical panic, but she still continued to babble incoherently about the unacceptability of the situation until he finally asked her whether she would rather return to the feeding frenzy of the paparazzi in London. And, not bothering to give her time to debate the question, he silkily added that, should that be the case, then escape might be tricky bearing in mind that they were thousands of miles airborne.

'We're sharing a house. It's a big house. Deal with it,' were his closing words before he slid his seat into its full-length bed position, donned some eye shades and fell asleep while she continued to fume and stew in silence for the duration of the plane trip.

It was, however, impossible to be argumentative with someone who, annoyingly, was refusing to be argumentative back. She sulkily buried herself in the guide books. She couldn't sleep. She actively resented the fact that he could. His lack of inner turmoil, his serene lack of conscience, set her teeth on edge. Once upon a time, they had been so united that it was as though their minds and bodies were fashioned to fit together. Time and again, the realisation that she had been mistaken about that barrelled into her, leaving her breathless and gasping.

And now, on top of that, there was the horror of having to share a house with him. She could have suggested the sensible option of renting a couple of rooms in a hotel, but she knew what his response to any such suggestion would have been.

She glanced across at his supine figure and found her eyes lingering on his long, powerfully packed body inclined away from her. He had kicked off his shoes and wasn't wearing socks. He had beautiful feet. She made an annoyed, strangled sound at the way her eyes treacherously strayed to him and then couldn't seem to unfasten themselves without a great deal of effort.

How on earth was she going to cope with the reality of being cooped up with him? How was she going to deal with the glaring comparisons between what they had now—this jagged, awkward relationship—to what they had once had, which had been so easy and laid back and, for her, redolent with promise? Sharing space with him was going to emphasise every painful detail of the road they had travelled down and the bitterly disappointing cul de sac it had reached.

Anxious thoughts kept her awake for the entire trip although it was only when the plane was about to land that Luiz stirred into wakefulness to slide his eyes across to where she was furiously reading yet another guide book, with her seat in its original upright position.

'No sleep?'

His rich, deep, velvety drawl made her start. His chair was back up and she glanced across to him. His dark hair was slightly tousled. He hadn't shaved and she could see that distinctive six o'clock shadow on his jawline. She used to find that unimaginably sexy.

'I wasn't tired.'

'In that case you obviously have a stronger constitution than me,' Luiz drawled lazily. 'The second I step foot on a plane, I'm always overwhelmed by an urgent need to sleep.

Unlike every other businessman I've ever met, I have no inclination to work when I'm up in the air.'

'Tell me about your house.' Holly had feverishly wondered how big it was. Every time she told herself that it was silly to be nervous about living with him, when she knew that he would be the perfect gentleman, she felt those vague panicky flutters and was uneasily aware that her greatest fear was of her own disturbing reactions to his presence.

'What would you like to know?' The plane was descending at a leisurely pace.

'How long has it been in your family?'

'A long time. It was always a convenient escape when we were in New York.'

'Right,' Holly muttered glumly, thinking how many things there were about him that had not come to light.

Luiz recognised that look on her face. It was the look she got when she was forced to accept the inevitable and the unwelcome. It was the look she had got when the geese had proved unsuitable and the challenge of re-housing them had morphed from possibility to certainty. Only after they had gone their separate ways had Luiz come to realise how much he actually knew about her and how intuitive his understanding of her personality was. But then, he had been helped by the fact that she had always been open and honest with him. She had been an open book and she had invited him to turn the pages.

In return, she had been rewarded with lies and deceit. A sudden surge of guilt rendered his voice harsher than intended. 'You needn't worry that you're going to have to hide from me,' he said tautly. 'The house is big enough for you to avoid my presence completely, if that's the road you want to go down. You'll be on your own quite a bit, anyway. This isn't time-out for me. I have work to do on the island and I'll be busy most of the time.'

'I never thought that I was going to have to hide from you.'

'You forget that I know you, Holly. I can read what you're thinking from the expressions on your face.'

'You *knew* me.'

'Eight bedrooms. Several bathrooms. At least a dozen reception rooms. A swimming pool. Path down to a secluded beach. Relax; you can lose yourself in the place.'

The plane was making its descent. Luiz had turned away and Holly wished she knew what he was thinking, the way he seemed to know what she was. How on earth had they got themselves into this mess? And how was it that she couldn't seem to rescue herself from it? She was at war with herself continually. Her hands still wanted to reach out and touch. Her body yearned towards his the way a plant twists towards the sunlight. Her mind still sought to slot in with his and find the old familiar places. And yet common sense battled valiantly to keep her responses under control. The effort was bewildering and exhausting.

She was dimly aware of the plane screeching along the runway and shuddering to a stop.

She had devoured all the guide books and already felt inured to what lay outside the airport and yet, stepping out into the sunshine, she realised that nothing had prepared her for the complete change of atmosphere and scenery.

'Speed isn't encouraged here.' Luiz was leading the way towards a taxi while she tripped along slightly behind him. 'Why rush?' He paused to allow her into the taxi and then slipped in alongside her and leaned forward to chat to the taxi driver, who seemed to know him. Questions were asked about Luiz and his family; his sisters had visited only six months ago…

Luiz introduced Holly and she smiled vaguely, feeling the disparity between their lifestyles rear up at her, but she was too engaged in staring around as the taxi pulled away to let negative feelings get the better of her.

She was aware that the taxi driver, whose name was George, was bringing Luiz up to date with gossip on the island and Luiz was laughing, murmuring that his mother would be thrilled to hear such and such and disappointed to know so and so.

He extended his arm along the back of the seat and Holly could feel it brush her hair, which she had scraped back into a ponytail as soon as she had exited the airport.

'How often do you come here?' She turned to him.

'Before I met you, a couple of times a year. Since I met you, not at all. I found that taking extended time out didn't hold quite the same appeal when the choice was mending a broken fence in darkest, coldest Yorkshire.' Their eyes tangled and Luiz shrugged. 'Now that we're best buddies, it's the truth, the whole truth and nothing but the truth—or something like that, from what I recall you telling me. I've always taken time out to return here but I didn't feel the need to when you were in the picture. Hence the hotel project hasn't progressed quite as quickly as originally anticipated.'

'I hope you're not going to blame me for that.' She stifled the quiver of pleasure she got from his admission that he had picked her over this place, then she immediately told herself that sex could sometimes be a compelling force for a man with a libido as rampant as his.

'No, Holly,' Luiz drawled. 'When it comes to the blame game, I'm the only one in the firing line, which is something else you've made perfectly clear.'

Holly flushed but, before she could say anything, he had moved on to something else and was coolly drawing her attention to the scenery around them, pointing out the picture-perfect pastel-coloured buildings and houses and telling her about the architecture, the limestone that was readily available and therefore used for construction at a time when it was too expensive to import alternative material.

Holly had expected the pastel-coloured buildings, the sub-tropical palms and the lush foliage, but she was still over-whelmed at the actual sight of all it. And the feel and the smell of it. It was a parallel universe, a Technicolor para-dise with the sun streaming down from a cloudless blue sky, pines and palms sharing space and buses lazily meandering along the winding roads.

'You think I never wanted to tell you about this slice of my life,' Luiz said softly as he stared at her delicate averted profile. 'But you're wrong.'

'Then why didn't you?' She wanted to tell him that ev-erything would have been different if he had opened up and told her the truth about him, except would it have been? A background grounded in massive wealth, a birthright of sus-picion and wariness and a catastrophic relationship with a gold-digger had cemented attitudes that couldn't be changed. 'Forget I asked that,' Holly said quickly. 'Have you, er, main-tained contact with the people here? Do you have friends on the island?'

Her mind wandered as he politely expanded on his experi-ences of the island. The sea glittered as the taxi swept along and Holly surfaced when she realised that it was turning off the small road and winding upwards. They had barely trav-elled any distance at all, really.

Immediately, she could tell that this was an expensive part of the island with its outcrop of impressive houses. The house to which they were heading and which finally sat squarely in front of them was a long double-storeyed house, surrounded on the ground floor by an enormous veranda, its lattice work entwined with clambering, colourful foli-age. Looking back, she could see that it enjoyed breathtak-ing views over sprawling gardens which were beautifully tended and bordered with all sorts of trees, some of which seemed almost European in origin.

'Wow.' Holly stepped out of the taxi and turned a full circle, eyes round as saucers as she took in the breathtaking scenery and slowly removed her thin cardigan which felt clingy and uncomfortable now that she was out of the air-conditioned taxi. The breeze was balmy, the heat just the right shade of comfortable. Turning back to the house, she saw a handful of people waiting to greet them. Luiz had brought next to nothing with him and he waited until of the young dark-skinned boys, smiling broadly, came to fetch the cases.

'Do you want to hear something really crazy?' Holly confessed shyly.

'I can't think of anything I'd rather hear than something really crazy…' The heat had put a glow in her cheeks and he could barely contain a fierce pride at the evidence of her pregnancy. His mother would have told the housekeeper who would have relayed the information down the ranks. They would all be aware that this was his woman and she was carrying his child.

'If I'd known you had all this when I first met you, I would never have gone out with you.'

Strangely enough, if any other woman on the planet had tried to pull that line on him, he would have burst out laughing, but he could reluctantly concede that she was telling the truth.

'And shall I tell you something really crazy in response?'

He was walking so close beside her that she could smell the heady scent of that familiar aftershave he always wore mixed with the masculine aroma of healthy perspiration.

'What is it?'

'Rumours of our friends-only relationship haven't quite reached my family's ears. I thought I'd save this information until we arrived rather than add to the list of misgivings you were concocting on the trip over.'

Caught in the act of taking the first step up to the broad, wooden veranda with its white wooden latticed railings, Holly stumbled in confusion as the gist of what he had said sunk in.

'What are you saying?'

Luiz slung his arm over her shoulder and drew her against him. All at once, Holly was so overwhelmed by the flood of familiar, unwelcome, heady longing that she could scarcely breathe. His muscular body was as hard as steel, rock-hard against her soft, pliable, softly rounded one. All the home help, watching this display of affection, were smiling. Luiz had had this house since for ever. Holly was sure that some of the home help would have been faithful family retainers since he was a child.

'I'm afraid I've spared my family the unpalatable fact that my pregnant mistress doesn't want to have anything to do with me.'

'That's not true!' Holly's jaw was aching from the effort of trying to smile effortlessly while conducting a *sotto voce* conversation which she suspected was only going to get worse.

'So everyone here is under the impression that we are, in fact, loved up and busily discussing wedding plans.'

'Why didn't you prepare me for this?'

'What do you think of the house?' Luiz smoothly diverted the conversation and there was a moment's reprieve as he stood back, turning to chat to some of the people clustered around him, leaving Holly to admire the cool, homely spaciousness of a house that had clearly been lived in and enjoyed by a family for many years. The wooden floors shone with the warmth of old patina; the rugs were faded, softly muted colours complementing the pale walls. The art looked local and there were framed pictures drawn and painted by children. Holly wondered whether any of those pictures were by a young Luiz.

For a short while, as she followed him and a couple of the boys carrying their cases, Holly forgot the contentious conversation they had just been having. Two of the older housekeepers, a couple in their seventies, were laughing and joking with him. Holly heard them but she was too absorbed in drinking in her surroundings to pay any attention to what they were saying.

The rooms were all big, airy and filled with light. The furniture was soft, worn and comfortable. They passed a number of reception rooms including a sports room equipped with a ping-pong table, a huge plasma television and general clutter.

She was determined not to be impressed; yet it was impossible not to fall in love with the place. And she hadn't even explored outside as yet, although the tangy, salty smell of the sea was filling her nostrils, wafting through the house on the balmy breezes, leading her to think that once she ventured into the extensive lawns and gardens it would be another case of love at first sight.

She snapped out of her pleasant reverie when they stopped in the doorway of a massive bedroom, dominated by a king-size bed and old-fashioned dark wood furniture. Voile curtains were gentle blowing in the soft breeze filtering through the opened shutters.

'We're here,' Luiz informed her drily. Without giving her time to vocalise the thoughts he could see shaping up in her head, he turned his back to her, murmured to the elderly couple, chuckled, then firmly shut the bedroom door, at which point he slowly turned to look at her.

'What do you mean, we're here?' Dismayed, she looked at the bags standing side by side in the bedroom.

'Like I said, the assumption is that we're loved up and, naturally, sharing a bedroom. Furthermore…' Luiz leaned against the closed door and stared at her, compelling her to look back at him until she could feel her mouth going dry in the intensity of the moment.

'Furthermore…?' Holly prompted weakly.

'Furthermore, my mother is in New York at the moment. She and my aunts visit the penthouse at least twice a year. Something about wanting to shop.' He allowed her to absorb that initial piece of information. He wondered whether she would join the dots and arrive at what he was about to say before he could get there himself. 'Naturally she wants to meet you and there's every chance that she will descend for a visit.'

'Luiz…'

'Did you think that my family would not want to meet the mother of my child at any point?'

'Your mother only wants to meet me because you've let her think that we're still…still…'

'A couple? Crazily in love with one another?'

*If only!* Holly laughed mirthlessly to forestall any cynical elaboration on that. Was he encouraging her to share the joke with him, that they could be crazy about one another? Despite everything she had said to him, did he know, deep down, that she was as crazy about him as she always had been? He was looking at her with a deep, dark, unfathomable expression and her skin prickled.

'I can't share this room with you.' Holly half-turned. Her pulses were racing and her nerves were all over the place.

'You can and you will,' Luiz said, his voice stony and implacable. 'I have known most of the people who work here for my entire life. Like my mother, they believe that this is a functioning relationship.'

'And that's your fault!' Holly cried, spinning round to face him.

Luiz shrugged with lazy indolence. 'What's the point in apportioning blame? This is how it happens to be at this moment in time. In due course, I will inform my mother that there will be no happy ever after but there was no way I felt inclined to break the news of her impending grandchild with the downside that the woman involved wanted no part in an ongoing relationship with me. Like I said, I come from a traditional family.'

'You're not being fair!' How was it that she had now become the bad guy? But, naturally, he wouldn't have confessed to his family that he had conducted a lengthy relationship with her under a pseudonym; that he had never considered her his equal; that they would never have been together had it not been for this unforeseen pregnancy...

All over again, the hurt rose up inside her, cutting through her composure and seeking to lay bare her vulnerability.

'I'm being truthful. If you migrate to another part of the house, you'll set tongues wagging here, and I'm not having that.'

'I should never have come here. It was a bad idea.' She tottered on shaky legs towards the rattan chair by the window. The thought of sharing a room with him filled every corner of her mind and made her feel faint.

'You're overreacting.' Luiz was by her in the blink of an eye. 'You've gone as white as a sheet.' He raked his fingers through his hair and squatted so that he was eye level with her. 'Try and understand that I'm protecting my mother from the bald truth of the situation for a short while.'

'Well, it won't take her long to figure it out if and when she meets me,' Holly muttered glumly.

'What do you mean?'

'She must know you, Luiz. She'd be daft not to work out

that someone like me is the last sort of person you would choose to be saddled with.'

Luiz was aware that he deserved that, yet there was no part of that observation he didn't find outrageous. He loathed the notion of her being hard and cynical about herself. Had he done that? He vaulted upright. She was tired. Stressed. The last thing she needed was another argument on the rights and wrongs of what he had done. Besides, on paper, didn't she have a valid point? Not as far as his mother was concerned, but certainly from the point of view of his overprotective sisters.

'I can't force you to share this space with me,' he granted grimly. 'But I'm asking.' He shoved his hands in his pockets and looked at her, his long lashes dipping over brooding midnight-dark eyes. 'The bed is big enough to fit a family of four. I will be away during the day. You can sightsee. By the time I arrive back home in the evening, you will probably have retired for the night. The old retainers here might raise their eyebrows at the lack of romance but they know me for a workaholic. They wouldn't be overly shocked, and at the end of the day we will only be on the island for a matter of a week or two.'

'And will your mother announce her arrival? Or will she just show up?' Under normal circumstances, the circumstances that had existed in her fantasy land before reality had taken its toll, Holly would have looked forward to meeting Luiz's friends and family. Now, she shuddered at the prospect of being judged by them. Would his mother think that she had got herself pregnant on purpose, to trap her rich, powerful, eligible and sinfully good-looking son into marriage? Would she think that he had escaped one gold-digger only, years later, to find himself skewered by another?

* * *

Nearly three weeks later, Holly would ask herself how she could have wasted so much time and energy fearing the possible arrival of Luiz's mother.

They had just seen Flora Casella into the taxi that would take her to the airport and return her to her daughters in Brazil. Like every other morning, the sun was already heating the island up, making sure that the sea breeze never got too chilly, turning the sprawling gardens surrounding the house into a breathtaking paradise.

Luiz's arm was slung loosely over her shoulder and Holly guiltily enjoyed the familiarity of its heaviness.

Flora Casella had come the day after they themselves had arrived at the island. Holly was sure that, not only had Luiz known exactly when his mother would be arriving, but had specifically chosen to keep the reality of their situation under wraps to buy himself time with his parent. She had grudgingly agreed to go along with the 'loving couple' charade and now…

Now, the charade would have to come to an end.

'Well?' Luiz murmured, his breath warm against her ear. 'Admit it. That wasn't too bad.' He turned her to look at him. The sun had turned her face a honey gold and brought a sprinkling of freckles out that hadn't been there before. She radiated sexy good health. Her hair shone. Her eyes gleamed. Her full, rosebud mouth was gratifyingly parted to receive his kisses. He trailed his finger along her chest, tracing the top of her dress and following it to where it dipped in a V between her breasts, which were so much bigger than before. He knew because he had buried himself in those breasts every night since they had shared that bed. He felt the drag of his senses as once again his libido began its routine of going into crazy free-fall simply at the memory of her luscious, naked body.

She had stopped fighting him. She had stopped pretending that there was nothing left between them. She had finally accepted that the chemistry still sizzled and fizzed. Things, he conceded, could not have gone better and all because she had come to her senses. It had taken an island and his mother to get her there, but she had got there and, really, who cared what journey she had taken to reach the destination?

'Shall we go inside?' His voice was a soft whisper against her skin. It made her shiver. She knew exactly what he meant when he asked that question. Her body was already preparing itself for their love-making. Each and every pore and nerve-ending was readying for his passionate onslaught. But his mother had left and the questions Holly had been asking herself, the questions which had temporarily been put to bed, were now stretching, limbering up and demanding answers.

Where was this going? She knew exactly what she had done when she had climbed into bed with him. She knew that she had just cracked, given up the pretence of hating him more than loving him. She knew that she had used his mother as an excuse and yet, in a way, it was his relationship with his mother that had done its job in demolishing her already crumbling defences. How could she carry on holding him at arm's length and telling herself that he was the enemy when the three-dimensional guy was a loving and considerate son? How could she cover her ears and pretend not to hear him when he fussed round his mother and was no longer the monster she wanted him to be?

She realised that she had used an argument that she had only been able to very weakly justify. She had mentally shrugged her shoulders and asked herself, well, why not? Why not enjoy him for a brief window in time? She had told herself that her attraction to him was a powerful urge that would work its way out of her system once she had slept with him, once she had stopped denying its existence.

She had stopped thinking about England and all the decisions that would have to be made. That felt like a different planet, far removed from the tempting balmy breezes, the amazing scenery and the warm, blue sea. How on earth was she supposed to stand firm when she was sharing a bed with him? She had found herself plunged back to that heady time when he was the only thing she could think of. How was she supposed to stand firm and resist when she was so far removed from reality, when there was nothing to distract her, when he was the only thing in their little garden of paradise? When it was just so easy to give in and when the smiling, warm approval of his mother made it impossible for her to rock the boat?

And, underneath all that, the truth was that she just couldn't resist the living, breathing man who was the devoted son willing to do anything for the mother he clearly adored. The lying, deceitful cardboard cut-out had gone, replaced by the guy she had never been able to walk away from.

But what happened now?

She now told herself that, just as soon as they started their journey back to England, she would address all those awkward questions in her head, because nothing had changed. He still didn't love her. Not once had that word crossed his lips although he never tired of telling her how much he wanted her. It had been a luxury to give in to him and to all the inconvenient impulses she couldn't get rid of, but the unpalatable truth that had compelled her to refuse his dutiful marriage proposal was still there.

'Go inside and do what?' She heard the teasing, sexy invitation in her voice with a twinge of guilt.

'I've given all the housekeepers and garden staff the afternoon off.'

'Why would you do that?'

'Because I've spent the past couple of weeks fantasising

about seeing you naked and in all your glory outside, by the pool with the trees casting shadows over you…'

'That's very poetic, Luiz.' But her breath caught in her throat and she fiddled with the little gold chain with the turquoise stone around her neck. His mother had given it to her on the very same day she had confided that she had had doubts about meeting her, but that those doubts had been dispelled within minutes because she could see how much her son loved her. Because a mother could tell; a mother could sense these things.

Holly had taken the necklace, slipped it around her neck and refrained from saying that love was the one thing Luiz didn't feel for her because if he did he would never have walked out on her; would never have assumed that their relationship was over the second she discovered who he was; would not have leapt into a relationship with a woman he considered more suitable weeks after they had broken up. She refrained from pointing out that he would have proposed marriage for a reason other than the fact that she had shown up pregnant at his office, thereby forcing him into the position of having to do the right thing. She diplomatically avoided mentioning that men in love didn't propose because it was a last resort and they couldn't see another way out.

'Perhaps you bring out the poet in me.' He laughed but there was a certain amount of surprise in his laughter, as though the thought, which should have been crazy, was maybe astonishingly bang-on target. 'A man in the company of his pregnant woman can sometimes discover he's a poet, against all odds.'

Holly wished he hadn't spoiled the illusion by bringing it back to sex but he was casually obliterating her common sense by slipping his finger under the spaghetti strap of her sundress, easing it over her shoulder, then doing the same to the other.

'No need to look around,' he murmured. 'Like I said, we're perfectly alone here. There's no one to see if I do this…' He tugged the dress down to her waist, where it precariously settled underneath her satiny, smooth stomach. 'God, you're beautiful,' he groaned in a husky undertone. The swell of her stomach was the most seductive and erotic thing he had ever seen, and that was saying a lot, considering he had never once found anything remotely sexy about pregnant women.

The land surrounding the house, usually busy with a team of gardeners, was silent and peaceful. The sound of birds and insects was faintly melodious. In the distance, the sea was a background noise, a lullaby. He cupped her breasts and his arousal hardened as she closed her eyes and drew in a shaky breath.

'I think your breasts are more sensitive now that you're pregnant.' He rolled his thumbs over her nipples and controlled the familiar urge to rush things along to accommodate the arousal pushing impatiently against his zip. 'Although, in fairness, you've always had sensitive breasts. That little pulse in your neck goes haywire when I do this to your nipples…and when I suck them…'

'Stop talking,' Holly begged. He had a line in sexy talk that could turn her to jelly.

'You prefer a man of action. That's good. Because I'm an action guy.'

'We can't do this here; we're still on the drive…anyone can come…'

'No one's going to come, and the house and grounds are completely private, but so what if someone came and saw me making love to you right here? They would get out pretty damn fast. But, if you don't feel comfortable here, shall we adjourn to the swimming pool? Perfect if you want a dip afterwards. Always nice to cool down on a hot day, especially when you've been exercising...'

'It *is* quite hot...' She was accustomed to her new proportions. Once upon a time, she might have been self-conscious about her slightly protruding belly, the fullness of her already big breasts, but the way he looked at her, the way he openly enjoyed caressing her stomach whilst marvelling at the miracle of life happening inside it...She blushed and giggled as he held her hand, leading her away from the front of the house, around the side and out towards the back where the infinity pool glittered bright blue and mouth-wateringly tempting.

'Okay...' Like a Roman pool, there were columns with flamboyantly coloured flowers curling and twisting upwards and Luiz leaned against one of the columns and grinned at her.

Holly blinked and thought that he truly was the most stupendous human being she had ever seen in her life. Nearly three weeks in the sun had lent his skin a rich, burnished gold, deeper and darker than in England.

'I love my mother,' he drawled. 'But she was a little too effective when it came to being a chaperone.' He slowly unbuttoned his shirt, shrugged it off and watched the helpless flare of desire light her eyes with a kick of primal satisfaction. 'What's the point of having this secluded house if I can't have my woman wherever and whenever I want her...?'

'That's so chauvinistic.' But her heart was beating wildly just at the thought of them making love wherever and whenever.

'So I'm a caveman when it comes to you. Tell me what's wrong with that? And, speaking as a caveman, I don't like the dress on you. Take it off and let me show you how a caveman behaves when there's no one around to see.'

# CHAPTER TEN

Luiz had dropped all talk of marriage. Expert at reading unspoken signals, he had sensed her immutability on the subject. Get past all the reasons she had come up with—all of them flimsy in the face of a pregnancy, as far as he was concerned—and he was still left with the fact that she was prepared to dig her heels in and adhere to her decision like glue, come what may.

But he hadn't counted on the paparazzi. He hadn't banked on her getting along with his mother like a house on fire and so falling in with his heartfelt request that she uphold a charade for a couple of weeks. Yes, he had known that she still wanted him, but the ease with which they had fallen into bed had come as a pleasant surprise and the past few weeks had cemented his conviction that marriage was inescapable.

And he felt good about that. Extremely good. Although, weirdly, introducing the subject seemed a much more delicate task now than it had when he had originally proposed. Back then, he had offered marriage with the casual assumption that she would accept. He could have been offering her a lift somewhere or a meal out. Now, he felt the need to tiptoe round the subject and was rocked by the notion that he might just be afraid. Afraid that she would turn tail and run away if he pushed too hard. How was it that fear could be part of his make up? Since when was he a guy who was scared of anything?

She was slowly removing her dress, stepping out of it, and he watched with that familiar stirring in his groin as her wonderfully lush, fertile and now pregnant body was revealed. The evidence of his own virility never failed to give him a high. Was he that vain? He just knew that he loved her slightly swollen stomach. He could lie with his hand on it for hours. He frequently found himself projecting into the future, wondering what his child would look like, what his or her personality would be. In fact, never had his imagination been so active, although that was something he would never have admitted to a living soul, even under pain of death.

Holly stepped towards him, her eyes locked with his. Still lounging against the column, Luiz tugged her gently to him and felt her melt in his arms as he lowered his dark head to take her mouth in a long, dragging kiss. Still kissing her, he straightened so that she could unbutton his shirt. He felt her smooth small hand linger over his chest. She circled his flat, brown nipples with her fingers and he pulled her closer.

'Your stomach gets in the way now,' he murmured raggedly.

'Do you mind?'

'Mind? I like it.' He dipped his hand over the bulge and then lower, trailing his fingers over the patch of soft, downy hair between her thighs. On cue, Holly parted her legs very slightly so that his roving hand could find that place. She arched back with a soft moan as he slipped two fingers between the folds of her femininity and very gently began to rub her sensitised clitoris which throbbed and pulsed as ripples of pleasurable sensation began to build.

'I worry that intercourse might not be a good idea at this stage,' Luiz murmured and she struggled to answer, fighting down the urge to succumb fully to the orgasm waiting for her.

'Don't be silly.' He was as naked as she was, although she couldn't recall him removing the remainder of his clothes, and she took his massive erection in her hand and played with it until she could feel him keeping the same wild impulses at bay as she was.

There was a magnificent, utterly decadent canopied bed under the shady patch of trees by the pool and they stumbled across to it.

Holly thought that the open air on her skin was absolute bliss. Not even in summer in Yorkshire, with the peaceful countryside around them, had they made love outside. This felt perfectly natural. This made her think that the human body was at its best without the impediment of clothes.

She lay down on the bed, which was really an outdoor mattress over which a huge fresh beach towel and piles of luxurious cushions were laid every morning, and she sighed with pleasure as he began his exquisite exploration of every inch of her body.

When she tried to interrupt so that she could pleasure him the way he was pleasuring her, he gently but firmly pushed her back against the cushions until she finally relinquished herself totally to his ministrations.

He sucked on her nipples until she couldn't bear it any longer, until she wanted to explode with the urgent craving to have him in her. He teased her by easing away only to resume his onslaught, licking and suckling and running his tongue over the distended buds.

'Feel free to make as much noise as you want,' she was aware of him saying at one point, and she really couldn't help the increasing tempo of her groans as his attention left her throbbing breasts and moved lower, to the silky honeyed smoothness between her legs.

She writhed and squirmed as he slid his tongue over and into her. She could no longer see his dark head moving between her thighs, but she could see his strong hands on her hips and the motion of his body as he continued to lavish his attention on that part of her that could never get enough.

Holly's fingers curled into the beach towel and she groaned and closed her eyes, lifting her body up to enjoy every second of his hungry mouth on her. She was so wet that she could hear the slick sound of his tongue grooving an inexorable path until she could feel herself reaching the point of no return.

She desperately wanted him in her, but she couldn't stop the orgasm as she came against his mouth, arching up and crying out as wave upon wave of sensation lifted her and carried her away. When she finally returned to planet Earth, it was to find him grinning at her before he stretched out next to her.

'You're very bad,' she admonished. 'I wanted you to come in me…'

'I know you did,' Luiz returned lazily. 'And I will. We have the whole day. There's no need to rush anything…' He turned so that he was lying on his side and he idly began to toy with her nipple, licking his finger and stroking the erect bud, marvelling at its immediate response.

If Holly could have held on to this moment and captured it for ever in a bottle, she would have. She knew that there were things to discuss: when would they be returning to England? What was going to happen when they had left this bubble and resumed life in the real world? She wanted to postpone all those difficult questions that would demand awkward answers for as long as possible but she thought that if she let him be the first to introduce them then she would somehow lose whatever control she had at her disposal.

But it just felt so good here, naked with him next to her,

playing with her breasts like a child playing with his favourite toy.

'You're falling asleep on me,' he chided with amusement
and Holly drowsily opened her eyes and smiled.

'I'm relaxed.'

'We need to talk. You know that, don't you?'

'Yes.'

'I'm going to go inside and get us something cold to drink,
things to snack on. Wait here for me.'

'Where do you imagine I could go?'

'True. My prisoner. I like it.' He hopped off the bed and
Holly watched as he made for the pool and dived in, swimming two lengths under water, his brown body slicing
through the water with speed and agility. It was mesmeris-
ing watching him.

He vaulted out of the pool in one easy movement, grabbed
a towel from the neat stack on the poolside table and shouted
over his shoulder that he could feel her watching him. There
was a grin in his voice.

With him gone, Holly lay back and worried about the
conversation that was on the cards. What were his plans for
the future? His mother was no longer around so there was
now no need to talk about marriage, which he had done previously, skirting expertly around the subject, managing to
imply rather than assert.

She sighed and her eyelids were fluttering shut, as the
warm breeze began returning her to her previous state of
contented drowsiness, when she heard the insistent ring of
his mobile phone.

She reached for his shirt without giving it a second's
thought. Without bothering to open her eyes, she lay back
to take the call but there was no one at the end of the line.
She could hear breathing but nothing else. She ended the call

and hadn't had time to slip the phone back into the pocket of his shirt when the text message came.

Holly sat up. Her pulses raced. Her contented drowsiness was scattered to the four winds at the sight of a woman's name: Claire. No doubt she had been the mystery breather down the other end of the phone. Who was Claire? Someone on the island? He had spent most days out at site. A few times, she and his mother had met him for lunch, dragging themselves away from the soporific laziness of just pottering in the house and escaping to the pool, but most of the time he had been out all day on his own. Was Claire an old acquaintance? Someone he worked with?

And, more importantly, wasn't this the very reason why their relationship was destined for a dead end? Because she knew that he didn't love her and so would still see temptation lurking around every corner. Doubtless whoever Claire was, it was all perfectly innocent, but she imagined herself with him, worrying that she might be getting on his nerves, that the fierce physical bond between them was waning; wondering whether his eyes were beginning to wander...

Belatedly, it occurred to her that if the mystery caller was a work mate she would have spoken at the other end of the phone rather than stay silent and send a text message.

She itched to read the message but knew that she wouldn't. Firstly, that would have been an invasion of privacy. Secondly, did she really want to read what had been written?

Her defences were up by the time he returned carrying a tray on which were piled biscuits, cheese and a jug of lemonade which she knew his mother had made for them the day before.

The warm sun no longer felt quite so good on her naked body and she reached for her discarded clothes.

'You make a better sight without the clothes.' Luiz sat

next to her and tugged the strap of her sundress but this time she felt herself stiffen.

'It feels weird to have a serious conversation without anything on.'

'Then we'll try to keep it light.'

'How can we? I mean, now that your mother's gone, there's no need for us to…to…pretend.'

Luiz stilled. He had been on a high. He had just brought her to a very satisfying climax and he was looking forward to spending the rest of the day repeating the exercise in as many varied ways as he could imagine. For once he wasn't itching to get back to London and the hive of activity. But in the space of twenty minutes something had changed and right now change was the last thing he wanted. He had planned on bringing up the whole marriage thing. He had been sure that she would no longer fight him on the subject he would use whatever convoluted means at his disposal not to scare her away. It was so good between them now. He was sure she would scc things his way, but the way she was studiously avoiding his eyes…

'Okay. Spit it out.' He reached for his shirt and slipped it on without bothering to do up the buttons. Then his shorts. Tension radiated in his body even though he told himself that there was nothing to worry about.

'Spit what out?'

'Whatever you're thinking that's suddenly changed your mood.'

'I guess it's time we both decide how we get on with our lives when we return to reality. I feel terrible that you'll have to let your mother down but I guess you can do it gently over time.'

She wondered what Claire looked like. She tried not to let her mind be taken over by suspicion. Part of her strongly longed to forget that she had ever taken that phone call and looked at the name on the screen. But she had to accept that any woman making an open and straightforward phone call would have spoken to her.

'How we get on with our lives…' Luiz felt as though he had taken a blow to his stomach. He couldn't breathe properly.

'We've shoved that to the back but we'll need to discuss all of that. When shall we leave, for instance? I guess the sooner the better. In fact, I think it's time I went to pack…' She had to get away. She felt like she might start hyperventilating. And she couldn't bear his eyes on her, sucking her back in. She grabbed her things and began hurrying into the house.

'What the hell is going on here?' He couldn't believe that this was happening. How could he have read the situation so wrong? He felt sick and no longer in control of events. 'Correct me if I'm wrong, but I was under the impression that things were good between us.' He had to make an effort to keep his voice steady as he followed in her fleeing wake. 'Or were you acting the whole time for the sake of my mother? Were you acting just now, when you were moaning and begging me not to stop? Or was that one last session for the road?' He wanted to pull her towards him, make her stop picking up bits and pieces that were lying around the house. He realised that his hands were shaking.

In the act of snatching up a hairbrush which she had left on a window ledge, Holly turned to stare at him. 'I wasn't acting!' she protested on a surge of anger. 'I've enjoyed the past couple of weeks and I…I don't do *last sessions for the road!* That's an awful thing to say. I was just raising the subject. *You're* the one who was keen to have this conversation.'

'I was keen to talk to you. This just isn't the conversation I had in mind!' *Why,* he wanted to yell, *are you doing this to me?*

Holly looked at him speechlessly and headed for the stairs. She should have known that she would have to pack and leave some time. So why had she managed to leave stuff in all four corners of the house? Had she been obeying some weird, subconscious urge to mark her territory? 'What did you have in mind?' she asked tightly. A tee-shirt was hanging over the banister. She grabbed it to add to the collection already in her arms.

'I was going to…' He shook his head and looked away for a few seconds.

The hesitation in his voice prompted her to look around, even though she knew that seeing him was dangerous. 'Going to…*what?*'

'It's crazy for us not to be married,' he said roughly. 'The past few weeks has proved that we could make it work.' He cursed silently to himself. Was this his idea of a gentle build-up? Something persuasive that wouldn't scare her off? Where had his talent for diplomacy gone?

Holly thought of that phone call. It filled her head and made the backs of her eyes prick with unshed, miserable tears. 'This was just pretend,' she said shakily. 'For your mother's sake. Okay, we fell into bed—I'm not denying that we…that there's still something there between us—but, like I said, it's not enough.'

'We've had a good time. *I've* had a good time. I've always had a good time with you.'

Holly had to strain to hear what he was saying. His voice was rough and defensive, challenging her to keep up the argument, but she was exhausted and unwilling to go over old ground.

'You'd get sick of me,' she told him bluntly, wearily making for the bedroom to dump her randomly collected possessions on the bed, before reluctantly looking at him. 'And then where would we be? I wouldn't be able to trust you not to…go off with someone else. And I don't care how much marriage makes sense, I could never live with that.'

'How can you assume that?'

*Because you don't love me and we're just back to square one talking about this.*

'You've been happy. I've seen it in your eyes. We can be happy together. I know it.'

'For a while, maybe,' Holly conceded tightly. 'But long-term? I don't even trust you now!'

'What does that mean?'

'It means that I don't really know what you get up to behind my back!' She folded her arms and could feel her nails digging into her forearms. To still her shredded nerves, she reached for her suitcase which was in the bottom of the vast wardrobe.

'Where the hell is that coming from?'

'It's coming from the fact that you had a call! Okay? Someone *called* you!'

'I'm not with you. What are you talking about?'

'Some woman called and then left a text message. Check your phone—go on, have a look—Claire. How can I ever trust you when you're getting calls from women who refuse to talk when I answer the phone?'

Holly heard the hysteria in her voice and wished she could have damped it down but her overwrought nerves—and, face it, biting jealousy—made that impossible. He had pulled out the phone from his shirt pocket, was flicking it open to read the message. She couldn't bear the thought of watching his face shadow with guilt.

'We're not an item,' she bit out. 'And you can do whatever you want with…with whoever you want. But don't stand there and talk to me about happiness. Don't try and make me believe that there's something special between us!'

'You really don't trust me, do you?' Luiz said quietly. He

looked at her in silence 'Okay. You win. We'll be off the island by this evening and when we return to London I'll get my lawyers working on a deal.'

What was the point of trying to win her back when she didn't trust him? He couldn't fight that. It would be like fighting shadows. Emotions he barely recognised were swirling inside him and his pain was something hard and physical and unbearable. He felt like a man suddenly and inexplicably deprived of his bearings.

Holly watched him walk away from her. Something about the angle of his head... Panic flared inside her. So this was finally it. She was getting what she had asked for. He was disappearing from her life and would resurface only to have a relationship with their child. She had succeeded in pushing him away.

She heard the slam of the front door before she finally realised that this was the worst possible way for things to end between them. She was sick of listening to her inner voice telling her not to cave in to a man who didn't love her. She didn't want to be torn apart with jealousy. She wanted to trust him because, yes, they had been happy.

Would he really have had the time or the energy to conduct a clandestine affair with a mystery woman? Common sense told her no. Whatever box she wanted to paint him into, Luiz would not have an affair with anyone while he was sleeping with her. He wasn't built like that. More than anything else, seeing his interaction with his mother, watching the way he slowed his pace for her, had shown her the complete man and that man was a man she could trust.

She didn't give herself time to think. She thought that he might have driven off somewhere, but his car was still parked in the shady area outside. Her thoughts were all over the place as she hurried down to the pool to find it still and empty. She was on the verge of giving up when she spotted him, sitting on one of the wicker chairs on the veranda at the back of the house. He was slumped forward, staring down at the wooden slats, perfectly still. He looked...vulnerable.

'I'm...I'm sorry.' Hesitantly, she stepped towards him. He hadn't bothered to look at her and she wondered whether she had truly blown her chances with him. She was terrified that she had. Hurt, pride, disillusionment... All seemed far away and insignificant when placed next to the loneliness of life without him in it. She took a deep breath.

'I know things are probably over between us, but I'm sorry. I *do* trust you. It's been hard for me. Hard to deal with the thought that we would never have got back together if it hadn't been for the fact that I fell pregnant. I was so madly in love with you, Luiz, and when you left I really thought that my bitterness would be bigger than my love. But it wasn't, even though I really, really wanted it to be. I didn't want to marry you because I just wanted you to want me for the same reason I wanted you. The same reason I'll *always* want you.'

Her legs were threatening to give way but he was looking at her now. She dragged one of the chairs over and sat down heavily. 'I want you to love me back,' she said simply. 'But, if you can't do that, then I'm willing to marry you because I don't think I can live without you. That's what these past two and a half weeks here have made me realise. If it's too late for us, if your marriage offer is off the cards—and I wouldn't blame you if it was—then I'll accept that.'

The silence seemed to stretch for ever. At last, he said, 'Claire Morgan didn't speak to you because I asked her not to.' He flicked through his phone and finally showed her a series of pictures of land. Open fields stretching out towards a distant horizon. Holly had no idea what on earth she was looking at.

'I wanted to surprise you. I've been working on this since we got here.'

'Working on what?'

'Claire Morgan is an estate agent. She must have panicked when she heard your voice. She's very young and new to the job and I may have been a little assertive when I stressed to her that the deal was for my ears only. Land for you—just outside London. And planning permission for you to build whatever house you want and, of course, have your animal sanctuary. All yours, if that was how it was meant to be, but mostly I wanted it to be a house for us.'

He looked at her and smiled with such tenderness that she felt her breath catch. 'Things happened. I was an idiot. I lied to you and...' He reached out and took her hand and stared at it as he fiddled with her fingers. 'I had made it my life-time's work never to let my heart get the better of my head because I was so wrapped up in making sure that I'd learnt my life lessons. I didn't realise that there are things in life beyond control and falling in love is one of them.'

'Falling in love?'

'I fell in love with a woman who loved me for someone without money or power or influence and I was so stupid that I never realised it. I walked out on the best thing that ever happened to me because I was convinced that the only kind of woman I could ever commit to would be to someone with her own fortune. I didn't want to let anyone in who could have an emotional hold over me. I didn't see that I already had.'

'So...you love me.'

'When you turned me away just now, I felt as though my world was falling apart. I wanted so badly to tell you how I felt, but I thought that, if you couldn't trust me after we'd been so close, then you'd never trust me. The hurt would always run too deep. But I love you so much. When I walked into your life, *crashed* into your life, I was someone broken and you...you put me back together. I was so stupid that I never even took time out to recognise that. I just carried on clinging to the crazy notions I'd built my life on and blundering about like a blind fool.'

Holly could feel herself welling up. She moved to sit on his lap and placed her hand just where she could feel the beating of his heart. 'You haven't been the only fool. I want us to build that house.'

'For us, my darling. A house where we can raise this child and all the other children that might come after. A family home. I want to devote my life to making you happy. And I hope you'll always let me...'

'Let you?' Holly gave a wobbly laugh. 'Just try and stop me.'

\* \* \* \* \*

**COMING NEXT MONTH from Harlequin Presents®**
AVAILABLE MAY 21, 2013

### #3145 THE SHEIKH'S PRIZE
*A Bride for a Billionaire*
**Lynne Graham**

Marrying Sapphire Marshall was the biggest mistake of Sheikh Zahir's life. Now, his ex-wife has returned to his desert and Zahir plans to banish her from his mind once and for all, beginning with reclaiming his wedding night!

### #3146 AN INVITATION TO SIN
*Sicily's Corretti Dynasty*
**Sarah Morgan**

Taylor Carmichael holds one thing precious: the reputation she's spent years rebuilding. Then one encounter with Corretti lothario Luca, a bottle of chilled champagne and a skin-tight dress and everything falls apart.

### #3147 HIS FINAL BARGAIN
**Melanie Milburne**

Eliza Lincoln is stunned to find Leo Valente at her door; four years ago his passionate embrace was a brief taste of freedom from her suffocating engagement. Now he's back, and he has a proposition he knows Eliza can't refuse....

### #3148 FORGIVEN BUT NOT FORGOTTEN?
**Abby Green**

Andreas Xenakis waited years to get his revenge on the DePiero family and now he finally has destitute heiress Siena at his mercy. But after just one night together everything Andreas believed about poor little rich girl Siena is shattered.

You can find more information on upcoming Harlequin® titles, free excerpts and more at www.Harlequin.com.

HPCNM0513RA

### #3149 DIAMOND IN THE DESERT
**Susan Stephens**

With the future of the Skavanga diamond mine in jeopardy, heiress Britt Skavanga needs an injection of cash—fast. She finds it in the mysterious Arabian investor known only as *Emir*...but his exacting fee is not financial!

### #3150 A GREEK ESCAPE
**Elizabeth Power**

Jilted by her cheating boyfriend, her self-esteem in tatters, Kayla Young escapes to an isolated Greek island. But the last thing she wants is to have to share her precious paradise with the mysterious, arrogant Leonidas Vassalio.

### #3151 A THRONE FOR THE TAKING
*Royal & Ruthless*
**Kate Walker**

Betrayed by those she loves, Honoria Escalona must face the only man capable of bringing stability to the kingdom of Mecjoria. But Alexei Sarova's past has changed him into someone she hardly knows, and his help comes with a price....

### #3152 PRINCESS IN THE IRON MASK
**Victoria Parker**

Dispatched by the king to retrieve his headstrong daughter, Lucas Garcia thought this was just another day at the office. That's before he meets Princess Claudine, who's adamant that returning to her father's kingdom is never going to happen!

HPCNM0513RB

# REQUEST YOUR FREE BOOKS!

**HARLEQUIN** *Presents*

PASSION GUARANTEED SEDUCTION

## 2 FREE NOVELS PLUS
# 2 FREE GIFTS!

**YES!** Please send me 2 FREE Harlequin Presents® novels and my 2 FREE gifts (gifts are worth about $10). After receiving them, if I don't wish to receive any more books, I can return the shipping statement marked "cancel." If I don't cancel, I will receive 6 brand-new novels every month and be billed just $4.30 per book in the U.S. or $4.99 per book in Canada. That's a saving of at least 14% off the cover price! It's quite a bargain! Shipping and handling is just 50¢ per book in the U.S. and 75¢ per book in Canada.* I understand that accepting the 2 free books and gifts places me under no obligation to buy anything. I can always return a shipment and cancel at any time. Even if I never buy another book, the two free books and gifts are mine to keep forever.

106/306 HDN FVRK

Name _____ (PLEASE PRINT) _____

Address _____ Apt. # _____

City _____ State/Prov. _____ Zip/Postal Code _____

Signature (if under 18, a parent or guardian must sign)

### Mail to the **Harlequin® Reader Service:**
**IN U.S.A.:** P.O. Box 1867, Buffalo, NY 14240-1867
**IN CANADA:** P.O. Box 609, Fort Erie, Ontario L2A 5X3

**Are you a current subscriber to Harlequin Presents books
and want to receive the larger-print edition?
Call 1-800-873-8635 or visit www.ReaderService.com.**

* Terms and prices subject to change without notice. Prices do not include applicable taxes. Sales tax applicable in N.Y. Canadian residents will be charged applicable taxes. Offer not valid in Quebec. This offer is limited to one order per household. Not valid for current subscribers to Harlequin Presents books. All orders subject to credit approval. Credit or debit balances in a customer's account(s) may be offset by any other outstanding balance owed by or to the customer. Please allow 4 to 6 weeks for delivery. Offer available while quantities last.

**Your Privacy**—The Harlequin® Reader Service is committed to protecting your privacy. Our Privacy Policy is available online at www.ReaderService.com or upon request from the Harlequin Reader Service.

We make a portion of our mailing list available to reputable third parties that offer products we believe may interest you. If you prefer that we not exchange your name with third parties, or if you wish to clarify or modify your communication preferences, please visit us at www.ReaderService.com/consumerschoice or write to us at Harlequin Reader Service Preference Service, P.O. Box 9062, Buffalo, NY 14269. Include your complete name and address.

HP13

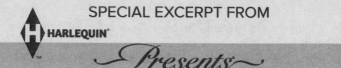
\* \* \*

"You barge into my life and proceed to conduct some sort
of military operation. And now you're going on like an
interfering, dictatorial knave!"

Suddenly Lucas stopped and turned on his heels to face
her. "Do you have an aversion to authority, Claudia? Is that
what this is? You don't like being told what to do?"

The gray silken weave of his tailored suit began to turn
black as the rain seeped through his clothing. His overlong
hair was already dripping and plastered to his smooth fore-
head and the high slash of his cheekbones. And the sight of
him, wet and disheveled, flooded her with heat. Like this he
was far more powerful and dangerous to her equilibrium.
He looked gloriously untamed.

"No, actually, I don't. Do you think it's right to force
someone against their every wish? To blackmail in order
to do your job?" Something dark flashed in his eyes, but
she was too far gone to care. "And because I dare to put up
some sort of fight, you deem me selfish and irresponsible.
Do you have any feelings?"

HPEXP0513-1

"I am not paid to feel," he ground out, taking a step closer toward her.

"It's a good job, 'cos you'd be broke," she replied, taking a step back.

Lucas pinched the bridge of his nose with his thumb and forefinger. "You're the most provoking woman I have ever met."

A mere two feet away, Claudia could feel the heat radiating from his broad torso. Oh God, she had to get away from him before she did something seriously stupid. Like smooth her hands up his soaked shirt. "You know what, Lucas? I'm staying here."

Before he could say another word, she bolted sideways. Only to be blocked by a one-arm barricade.

"Over my dead body," he growled, corralling her back toward the car.

\* \* \*

*Find out who will win the battle of wills in*
*PRINCESS IN THE IRON MASK by Victoria Parker,*
*available May 21, 2013.*

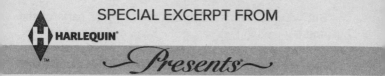

*The more powerful the family…the darker the secrets….*

*Read on for an exclusive sneak peek from*
*AN INVITATION TO SIN by USA TODAY bestselling*
*author Sarah Morgan, book #2 in the epic new miniseries*
*SICILY'S CORRETTI DYNASTY.*

\* \* \*

TAYLOR reminded herself that Luca Corretti was probably
the most dangerous man she could possibly have found herself with. "I thought you were trying to behave yourself."

"This is me behaving myself." He took another mouthful
of champagne, and she laughed in spite of herself, sensing a
kindred spirit. A part of her long buried stirred to life.

"So both of us are making a superhuman effort to behave.
What's your excuse?"

"I have to prove myself capable of taking charge of the
family business." Underneath the light, careless tone there
was an edge of steel and it surprised her. She didn't associate
him with responsibility.

That thought was followed instantaneously by guilt. She
was judging him, just as others judged her and she was better
than that.

"But you turned the House of Corretti around."

"I have a flare for figures."

"Especially when those figures belong to models?"

He laughed. "Something like that."

"But why do you want to meddle in other parts of the business?"

"Sibling rivalry."

"But you're all members of the same family. Surely that qualifies you for a seat on the board."

"The qualifications for a seat on the board seem to be old age and sexual inactivity." He suppressed a yawn. "I suppose that's why they call it a 'bored.' I have a feeling that whatever I do, I will always be in the wrong."

Taylor felt a flicker of sympathy. "I know that feeling."

"I'm sure you do. You, Taylor Carmichael, are one big walking wrong." His gaze lingered on her mouth. "So tell me what else is on your list of banned substances."

"Men like you."

"Is that right?" Somehow, without her even noticing how he'd done it, he'd moved closer to her. His dark head was between her and the sun and all she could see were those wicked eyes tempting her toward the dark side.

"What are you doing?"

"Testing a theory." His mouth moved closer to hers, and suddenly she struggled to breathe.

"What theory?"

"I want to know whether two wrongs make a right." His smile was the last thing she saw before he kissed her.

* * *

*Find out if sinfully attractive Luca's theory proves to be right in AN INVITATION TO SIN by Sarah Morgan. Available May 21, 2013, wherever books are sold!*